B Cyde Books presents

Murder on the Yard
The Black College Sabbatical 20 Years Later

Tracie E. Christian

Murder on the Yard – The Black College Sabbatical 20 Years Later

Written By: **Tracie E. Christian**

Edited By: **Tracie E. Christian**

Published By: **B Cyde Books LLC**

Cover Art By: **Tracie E. Christian**

ISBN – 13: 978-1-7356375-3-2

To learn more about Tracie E. Christian visit www.thebcyde.online **or Tracie E. Christian Author Pages on Amazon & Facebook**

Acknowledgements

This go around I am going to keep my acknowledgements short and sweet.

Lord and Savior Jesus Christ - Thank you for keeping me in sound mind and body to use this gift you have seen fit to give to me. I will never neglect it. Thank you for seeing me through storms to get me here! Let the Rain Come Down Indeed.

Michael Favors (My Husband) – Thanks for taking grand care of me in sickness and in health! Your push to write this book shows me how much you love and believe in my gifts. Thanks for being the Best Husband/Lover/Friend a Lady could ask for! Eternally in Love, Tracie

Imani E. Favors (My Daughter) – My greatest creation will always be You! Your cheerleading, pep talks and comedic breakdowns in retrospect always get me inspired. You are a dynamic young woman that I am proud to have as a daughter. You complete Me & I will love YOU Forever, Mommy Girl

Diane L. Christian (My Mommy) – In the words of the classic '70's Staples Singers jam, "Let's Do It Again"! I know I knocked your socks off when I wrote my first book, so writing my ninth now, I am so glad to have the biggest support system in you still with me! We had a rough year in 2020 but your light guides my path to greatness! The most precious gem in my possession is YOU Mommy! I Love You always & forever, Tracie – Your Baby Girl

Friends, Family & Foes: Thanks for your support or lack thereof. Either way it has fueled my fire in writing the best stories to entertain the masses and I appreciate your part in my career path. My SUCCESS could not be spelled without U! Love, Peace & Smooches!

Introduction

A Prayer from the New President
of Heritage State University
February 2021

Dear Lord,

As always, I am starting this prayer giving honor and glory to you! I am forever in awe of the blessings you have bestowed upon myself and my family. I could have never imagined the events of the last two years but as the old saying goes, "If you want to make God laugh, tell him your plans!" I started off just wanting to be the change in my life that I wanted to see. I wanted to be a better man of activism, integrity and influence for my family, my community and ultimately, my culture. You, of course, saw and led me far beyond that and now as I sit on the eve of my inauguration as the 10ᵗʰ President of Heritage State University, I am realizing a dream I never, in a million years, thought would ever come true!

Historically Black Colleges and Universities need so much and the one you have selected me to head up is no exception. Beyond my bright ideas, I am prepared for opposition. I know my platform in running for this position was centered around the concept of, Returning to an HSU of old. With that, I am aware that the folks who voted me in, are banking on a restoration of usual practices and forgotten tradition. While I will do my best to please, I am not in the business of appeasing! I am also aware that there is a mighty minority hell bent on advancing a migration to multi-cultural status in efforts to erase our school's historically black history. In short, I know I will be challenged and championed by our staff, students and school community at unprecedented numbers and turns. I will also need more support and effort from our administration and alumni than any of the presidents before me! I do not know what is in store for our future, however I have faith that you will always guide my decision making to encompass what is right and just in the best interests of our school and its students first.

I am energized, optimistic and excited about starting this new school year in a new role as leader of the university that gave me an education, a wife and has been a part of my family for over 20 plus years. Please continue to walk with me through this journey to become the first President of Heritage State University to make ground-breaking history!

In your name I pray,

Dr. Eric Smith PHD. Ed
Heritage State University President
HSU Class of 2001

Prologue
The Destruction of Destiny
A Celestial Perspective

It's Homecoming Week – 2021 at Heritage State University and limited, safety-oriented, socially distant festivities are in full swing. Tonight's Miss HSU Coronation is the quintessential event that sets the celebratory stage for the rest of the weekend. The school's most popular female is crowned the ultimate ambassador and this year's recipient is a candidate that has been bred for this position since the day she was born. Destiny LeLani Turner is an accomplished graduating senior, with a 3.4 grade point average. She is Captain of the Honey Squad with the HSU Marching Band, and an active member of Tau Delta Omega Sorority Incorporated. Destiny is a multi-legacy that has been on the campus Royal Court since her freshman year and now is her personal time to shine. As she prepares for the most important night of her college life, her parents and grandparents on both sides of her family are all excited, present and accounted for with bells on.

This year, Heritage State is the first historically black university to re-open its campus for a major event since the health crisis that shutdown the entire country in March of 2020. Although Howard University did open its campus for the 2021 Inauguration festivities with the new Vice President being an esteemed alum, all other HBCU schools moved to virtual learning with ghost town campuses closed to the student population at large, and the public. Although the Corona Virus pandemic led to the cancellation of the fall football season and largely restricted the basketball season, it is now supposedly safe for historically black colleges to go back to business as usual or at least, some variation of it and Heritage State is leading the pack. If all goes well, this could surely be the game changer this school needs to be considered a contender among the brightest and the best of historically black colleges and universities across the country. This homecoming weekend is a well-orchestrated, power move for Heritage's new president, Dr. Eric Smith and with any luck it will be the move that defines his presidency.

"There, now your make-up is picture perfect. Now remember to be careful bouncing about tonight. I had to use extra foundation your arms and back to hide those bruises in this dress so don't be brushing up against shit all will nilly!" Destiny's cousin that is more like a sister, Dream Turner announces softly as she dabs the final touches of blush on Destiny's flawless keen-featured, beige caramel face. "How'd you get those again?"

"I told you, helping my roommate Jazmeen move some heavy ass furniture out of her spot. You know I'm accident prone Cuzzy Wuzzy. Anyway, thanks Dream. It looks beautiful. God I am getting nervous. I hope nothing goes wrong Dream. Everything has just got to be perfect tonight. How is the crowd looking out there?" She asks, nervously trembling sitting in front of the mirror in a strapless, cream colored Cinderella style ball gown with metallic gold knit overlay accents. Her light-brown hair, with dusty, blonde highlights is swooped up into a neat bun as long, spiral curls lay at both sides of her head. Destiny is the picture of loveliness as she stares at Dream through the mirror's reflection with a look of sheer fright in her eyes.

"Don't worry you've got the packed house your mother has been striving for. And what could go wrong Cuz? You've got those minion Honey Groupies of yours jumping at your every command like they're pledging, and Auntie Cierra has been breaking necks trying to get everything you requested for this coronation and more. Everything is going to be fine, Destiny." Dream jokes just as both hers and Destiny's parents', Chavon and Kyla Turner and Cherod and Kayla Turner storm into the dressing room right outside the main entrance aisle of the auditorium.

"I'm just saying you did not have to park that far back in the parking lot Chavon. We're already late riding with your slow driving ass! We could have got here sooner if we would have just walked next to the fucking car." Kayla barks at her brother-in-law.

"Not if I run your ass down first Kayla." Chavon comes right back rushing past her to hold his arms open to his daughter, Dream as she resists.

"Hey there precious Niecy! You are looking amazing in that gown." Kyla compliments her niece as she hugs her daughter.

"Hey Auntie Kyla. Where's my?" Destiny starts after a quick hug and kiss with her aunt, but before she can finish her statement, her question is answered.

"Your lovely, successful, fly-as-fuck parents are right here baby girl!" Destiny's father, Cherod Turner announces with a huge smile spread across his peanut-butter colored, smooth face. As soon as Cherod gets directly in front of his daughter, he stops dead in his tracks. His eyes fill with water and red hues become visible in his cheeks.

"Daddy what's wrong? Don't I look okay?" Destiny asks panicked.

"Nothing is wrong Des. I just used to always wonder what it would be like to see the most beautiful girl in the world and…now I know."

"Aww, you said the same thing when you met her in the hospital when she was born, and when she graduated from kindergarten, and high school." Destiny's mother, Kayla offers sweetly with a hint of sarcasm, gliding into the room like a summer breeze, kissing her daughter as she pokes fun at her husband. The room erupts with laughter as they continue to greet one another. The air is warm with love, and the moment is sentimental as they prepare to watch one of their own be crowned HSU Royalty.

"We are all very, proud of you Destiny. This moment trumps everything I could have ever dreamed of for you Sweetheart." Destiny's Auntie, Kyla professes her sentiments so purely with tears in her eyes. Kyla was always like that with her niece. She was like a second mother to Destiny even after Kyla had her own daughter two years after Destiny was born. And although Kayla is just as close to Kyla's daughter, Dream there was always something extra special about the bond between Kyla and Destiny.

"Oh Lord, let's just all gather up and go find our seats in this auditorium before it becomes a fucking flood fest up in here." Cherod jokes as both Kayla and Kyla smother Destiny with hugs, love and mushiness.

"Hold on, where are my grandparents?" Destiny demands wiping tears away after hugging the ladies.

"Which ones?" Her dad's brother, Chavon jokes looking on.

"Both, Unc quit playing," she jokes back grinning at him as he tries to throw his free arm around Dream's neck. When she ducks and moves without words, he looks sad but brushes it off like its nothing.

"Both sets of elders, the Turners and the Mansfields are in the auditorium holding our seats. We just wanted to run back here to wish you luck and let you know how very, proud of you we are Destiny." Kayla gushes over her one and only as she removes stray hairs from Destiny's face with love all in her eyes. "You look beautiful, Darling."

"Thanks mom. Thanks everybody. This is a dream come true and you all helped to make it all possible. I am happier than I have ever been. Now yawl have got to get out of here before I mess up the makeup Dream worked so hard on crying." Destiny announces and with that sentiment, flowers and lots of hugs and kisses, both sets of moms and dads exit her dressing room. When they are sure the grown-ups are out of ear shot, the close net cousins continue talking.

"They are too much huh?" Dreams asks, shaking her head with a smirk.

"Girl yes. I am already nervous enough. All the sentimental stuff was sure to get to the water works going and I cannot have that. Not now."

"I feel ya Cuzzie! You cannot mess up one of my best make overs. Anyway, where are the fellas with that thing they are supposed to be carrying you out on? And what are you trying to do with an entrance like that anyway? Who are you trying to be The Queen of Zumunda or somebody?" Dream jokes referring to Destiny's idea for a *Coming to America* style coronation theme.

"That thing you're talking about is called a Sudan Chair, fool and no other black college campus queen has ever made a grand entrance like this before. It's gonna go down in HSU Homecoming History and blow their fucking minds." Destiny gushed. "The guys that are carrying me on it are on their way. I just got their text, and might I add that they each are the finest, most sculptured bodied brothers on the football team, all oiled up and representing every variation of mocha magic in every shade excellently. It's a good thing this dressing room is right outside the main aisle of the auditorium cause if it wasn't the girlies would gather with the quickness around the guys and forget all about me and you know I ain't even having that shit. As for your other questions you know damn-well I am not an ordinary Miss HSU so, I cannot have an ordinary coronation. I'm not exactly a fan of all the pomp and circumstance, but if I've gotta do it, then I am going to dare to do it differently than anybody else ever has, and take this shit back to the motherland, ya heard me!" Destiny professes with sheer delight on her face.

"Okay Des. I see your gangsta! Okay well I'm going to go grab my seat but before I go, I almost forgot to give you this." Dream says as she hands Destiny a green and silver giftbag.

"What's this Dream?"
"Look and see."

When Destiny reaches in the bag and pulls out a long white box, she is speechless. She opens it to find a glistening white gold charm bracelet. The charms are all meaningful symbols of Destiny's college experience; a star (representing her super student status), a ballerina (represents the Honey Squad), a charm spelling the word STEM (represents her major) and connected hearts (representing their connection). Destiny is unable to stop her tears as she examines her bracelet.

"This is just a little bling for our Campus Queen." Dream jokes.

"Dream its beautiful. I love it! Thank you!" she offers jumping up, hugging her cousin tightly over sniffles and tears.

"Alright, alright, that's cool, and you are welcomed but watch your makeup. Slide it on right quick cause I've got to go." Dream rushes Destiny as she breaks their embrace and leaves the room to watch her cousin make family history.

The scene in the auditorium is understandably awkward with a full house, spaced out and limited to 1/3 capacity thanks to Covid-19. Destiny's grandparents on her father's side, Rasheed and Gloria Turner are seated front row center, looking like money and black excellence in winter white outfits. Both in Armani suits and diamonds, her maternal grandparents, Michael and Jacqueline Mansfield look elegant, esteemed and accomplished in their all-black attire. Each pair represent polar-opposite sides of black affluence and it is a spectacle to watch every time. The pride on their faces speaks without any of them saying a word. As they sit together, visibly tolerating each other, while patiently waiting for the festivities to begin, the tension between the pairs is obvious to anyone looking. But, as promised to their granddaughters, each is on their best behavior to resist causing any kind of scene. No other scene can take place, not on this night, and not, here.

The stage is decorated beautifully with tall, gold potted plants of burgundy African Violets surrounding its perimeter, cleverly accenting everything maroon and white in the room. From the elaborately assembled gold archway to the decorative gold drapes that surround the stage and the Kente carpeted runner leading to the end of the stage everything is immaculate. From the center aisle of the auditorium to the rows of seats reserved for Mr. & Miss HSU's families and special guests, everything is regal and beautiful. There are also rows reserved for the HSU Royal Court with the next two rows reserved for families of the Royal Court. The entire scene is all very well-orchestrated and rehearsed. Destiny would settle for nothing less.

The air in the room is filled with that all too familiar alumni comradery and nostalgia as each set of grandparents have fond memories of this campus and even this auditorium. Michael and Jacqueline graduated from Heritage in this room, and Rasheed and

Gloria had the honor of watching their son, Chavon graduate from HSU in this room 20 years earlier. The legacy their granddaughters are continuing at Heritage brings much joy to the hearts of each.

The house lights slowly dim as Mr. & Miss HSU Chorus file onto the stage taking their designated seats next to the microphone on the right front corner. They sing a stirring rendition of The Lord's Prayer to open the ceremony. New HSU President, Eric Smith offers a riveting and inspiring welcome speech before sharing his own memories of the Queen-to-be as an inquisitive, busy little girl he calls his Goddaughter. Next, the Mistress of Ceremonies for the evening Cierra Folsom, HSU Band Auxiliary Coordinator, proceeds to introduce the Royal Court representatives for each college.

The flow of young men and women that glide in paired up representing their selected disciplines is impressive. With the men dressed in black tuxedos with white vests and neckties, and the ladies in maroon ball gowns with white accents it all looks like something out of a movie. The excitement of witnessing the crowning of the 100th Miss Heritage State University further intensifies with the introduction of the Queens Court represented by Mr. & Miss Freshman, Sophomore, Juniors and 1st and 2nd Mr. & Miss HSU Attendants. When the final couple take their rightful position on stage, it is time for the moment the entire room has been waiting on.

Jacqueline gazes over briefly at her eldest daughter, Kayla just to catch a quick glimpse of the motherly pride she is sure Kayla's eyes are displaying. Reminiscing about Kayla giving her that same feeling many moons earlier as the queen of their sorority, she is moved to quiet tears herself. Seeing her granddaughter being crowned in yet an even higher, more esteemed position is better than anything she could have ever wished for. In her mind, this moment could not be any better if it were written somewhere in book.

The steel drummers begin the intro cadence for the campus queen's processional. This ceremony's setting is as much cultural as it is traditional, however there are still unexpected elements that add to the fun of the festivities. Like the gasps and mild cat calls from men in the audience at first sighting of the young ladies throwing flowers leading the processional down the auditorium's center aisle. Their Kente cloth head wraps, sarongs and matching halter tops offering up a tasteful helping of leg, thigh and midriff action that excites every brother in the room. Pride is evident on all the elders faces as the spectacle unfolds. The school's male dignitaries are also dressed in tuxedos adorned with vests and ties that match the aisle runner. With the ladies draped in dresses of the same design, the entire scene is already better than any other coronation has been to date. It was important to Destiny that her coronation be a celebration of cultural excellence and majesty which is why she remained hands-on throughout the entire planning process. The devil of her high-class, culturally diverse upbringing, education and tastes are vividly displayed in every detail.

The whoops and hollers heard for the Flower Girls is nothing compared to the screams of the ladies at the sighting of the four, God-like bodied, greased up male specimens carrying that shiny, gold Sedan Throne on two long posts up high in the air on their shoulders, with a thick gold shimmering drape covering the campus queen as it starts its slow procession down the center aisle. When Kyla looks over at her sister, she and Cherod have tears trailing down the sides of their faces as the audience stands for the queen's entrance. She grabs her sister's hand totally caught up in the rapture of this grand occasion. She is just as happy for her niece as her sister is. The grandparents are elated, and her husband and brother-in-law are simply overjoyed with pride. Suddenly, in all the chaos and discord that usually surrounds this well-to-do family most times, it's a glorious moment for both the Mansfields and the Turners and the irony of the location for this minor miracle to occur, at Heritage State University, is not lost on any of them.

As the men carry the Sedan Throne down the aisle, the butterflies flutter furiously in Kayla's stomach as her husband, Cherod squeezes her hand when they pass them. She gazes down the row to see tears of joy streaming down the faces of all the ladies that love her daughter too. It's such a special moment in time that she will not ever be able to forget. Her mother blows a kiss at her, and her father winks his approval of her job well done in raising a sweet, respectful, accomplished young lady. For their entire family, this moment is everything and more. Once the men get the throne positioned on stage the Mistress of Ceremonies begins the Introduction and the HSU Coronation Decree. As she wraps up, the moment they all have been waiting for is only seconds away, the unveiling of this year's Heritage State University Campus Queen.

"We the administration of Heritage State University humbly present the 100th crowned, Miss Heritage State University 2021-2022, Destiny LeLani Turner!!!"

The audience erupts in applause as the spotlight zeros in on the throne and the gold drape covering the queen is removed slowly. The crowd is instantly hushed to silence when the image becomes fully visible of Destiny LeLani Turner, the newly crowned Miss HSU on that throne in the most beautiful crème and gold ballgown imaginable, with a bright red streak of blood running down the front of her gown from her sash. With her wrist bound to the sedan chair with electrical tape,

Destiny is unconscious and bleeding from the abdomen in front of the entire campus community.

Moments later the screams start as Destiny's entire family rushes the stage. The president orders for someone to notify the police and within minutes sirens can be heard in the distance. Security and university officials help ushering the audience out the auditorium as Kayla, Kyla their mother, Jaqueline and Destiny's paternal grandmother, Gloria Turner are all distraught attempting to tend to their baby until help arrives. Chavon Turner, Destiny's Uncle wrestles his brother's hands from around the neck of one of the muscle-bound guys carrying that throne.

"What the fuck did yawl do to my daughter! How did this happen to her! Who did this?" He screams at the top of his lungs and his anger, completely enraged. It takes everything in Chavon to remind his brother that boy is someone else's child as he stops Cherod from choking the boy out. He wants answers about his niece too, but he also knows assault is not the way to get it.

The paramedics quickly cut the tape and prep Destiny for her trip to the hospital. They attempt to revive her but the most they get is a weak pulse before piling her into the ambulance. They make it a point to alert the family that Destiny is going to need a blood transfusion once they get her to the hospital. Then Kayla, her sister and the grandparents all go to the hospital while Cherod and Chavon stay on the scene at the school with their friend, Eric Smith to see what the police come up with. The investigation lasts for hours.

Until this very moment, Homecoming 2021 was going expertly with great attendance, wonderful media coverage, fundraising at an all-time high and implementation of a well-designed public safety plan that is the first of its kind in this post-pandemic age. And still withstanding, despite episodes of small world drama, in an instance it is all ruined in less time than it took to lead a processional to the end of the goddamn aisle. This event is going to trump everything good that happened homecoming week. More importantly, how the university responds in its wake will be key to its success or demise. Plus, tomorrow is still Homecoming. There is a mass alumni meeting, the parade, the game and vendors hitting the yard and it is way too late to try to cancel. Now, on top of all that Heritage will have increased police presence too for homecoming because there has now been an attempted murder on the yard!

5 Days Earlier –
Heritage State University
The Beginning of
Homecoming Week 2021

Chapter 1
Let the Mind Games Begin
Dr. Eric Smith

I am up early as hell, taking an ultra-hot soak in this expensive ass Maya Bath Superior Steam Shower & Tub combo my wife, Tina insisted we have installed last year for our 20th wedding anniversary. Yep, while the house is still asleep, I try to find some solace. I know it sounds crazy how at 4:45 am, I find myself just sitting in the whirlpool full of water, trying to let the jets do their magic on my muscles. Although this thing is equipped with a 12" LCD TV screen, and Bluetooth connectivity, I sit with my eyes closed tight, in total silence.

I need this time to sort through some shit by myself. The earlier I get up, the longer my spa time gets these days. This pandemic is fucking up everything in my world right now and my stress level is at an all-time high. As if being in the house with my wife and two college-age children 24/7 for the better part of four months wasn't extra enough, I have had my head in so many Zoom, Skype and Microsoft Teams meetings over the last two months that it feels like my brain is going to burst. Working with my new transition team and the scores of folks involved in starting this new 2021-22 school year at my alma mater, Heritage State University off completely virtual was no easy feat. I am mad stressed with the pressures of my job, my kids' indifference to my plight aggravates the hell out of me, and to top all that shit off, I miss my damn wife literally, figuratively and intimately.

She has been out of town for the last two weeks at a book conference and when she did finally come home, we did not connect like we used to. Instead, we had a huge debate over our quality time as of late, or as she put it, the lack there of and it did not end well at all. Slammed doors and raised voices screaming points of view neither one of us is listening to won over the common sense and compassion we normally have for each other. We have not said more than two words to each in four days and I would be lying my ass off if I didn't admit that our couple issues are at the fore front of my mind too.

She startles me back to alertness when I hear the Bluetooth connect to someone's phone, because mine is still changing in our bedroom. Seconds later the bathroom lights dim, and the door slowly starts to open. My wife appears in the threshold of the bathroom wearing her white terry cloth robe. She closes and locks the door behind her after entering and I am immediately hopeful for something sexy happening next, but remembering our fight, I quickly calm the fuck down.

Even in shadows, Tina's beauty is undeniable. Twenty-four years after meeting her, she still takes my breath away. I turn to look at her and we say nothing. With sensuality all in her glances, she unties the belt of her robe. Allowing it to fall to the floor, her naked, peach complexioned, smooth, well-tone runner's physique is on full display and I cannot take my eyes off her. Her long auburn and brown straight hair trails down her back with two thick strands over her shoulders on either side, barely covering her round plump, nipples.

The slow six steps she takes to the tub is all it takes for my manhood to jump to attention.

We have not made love in weeks and like I said earlier, I fucking miss my wife. At this moment I would gladly declare her the winner of every argument known to man if she will just let me lay her down. With water just below the top of the tub, she opens the tinted glass door and steps in with me. She tries to say something, and I stop her. So glad to finally have her this close to me she does not need to say anything. I cover her lips with one finger as I scoot up to her, grabbing her around the waist and pulling her towards me with the other hand. She barely gets situated straddling me in the tub before I am deep, inside of her. In no time without words, we are ravishing one another. Her hands move wildly over my bald head as I guide her body carefully up and down my shaft as slow as possible. I feel her walls grip my stiffness with every stroke and I take my time, wanting to prolong this moment for an eternity if I can. Her stares of passion are intoxicating.

"I'm so sorry for our fight," she whispers in my ear as she rides me.

"Me too. You know I love you, Tina. I hate it when we fight. Loving you is my specialty babe."

"Oh, yes Baby," She moans out as I finesse her to her first orgasm, and she collapses onto my chest. Just getting started I hold her tightly gripping her ass and slowly, grinding more circular strokes into her earth. Within minutes she squirts again, and it makes me climax with her. After catching our breath, Tina soaps up a loofah and begins lathering my body across my aching shoulders and back.

"Here let me help my baby relax," she offers sweetly rubbing my back with the loofah drenched in lavender body gel.

"Thanks baby. I've got a busy morning ahead of me today. The vote for the Capital Campaign proposal is this morning and I need to get to the office early, so I can finish reviewing the terms of both proposals. I want to make sure I understand everything about each of them crystal clear." I explain as I enjoy all the special treatment.

"What's there to understand? The proposal the Board of Trustees are pushing requires the school to ramp up diversity recruitment, advocating for more non-African American students. If left up to the Board Heritage won't even look like an HBCU anymore much less operate like one."

"Babe there is more to it than that. Our enrollment has been on the decline for years. A multi-cultural related approach to recruitment aligns us for more federal grant money. I must consider all viable options to change the narrative. Hell, it's my job to!" I announce as I turn to face her. The rub down stops, and the mood has switched from tender to tempered in moments. The look of disapproval is etched on her face like stone.

"Your job is to make decisions that will best impact to entire school community. Not just foster the notions of a small majority." She insists heatedly.

"That small majority, as you call it, is the governing body for the entire university Tina! This fight was started before I even took office. The Board is deadlocked, and I have the deciding vote! This one is a decision I can't afford to make emotionally, Love." I tell her with a sincere need for her to take her emotions out of this conversation too. I know her ties to Heritage run deeper than most, but this is not about her. "I have to consider all options before making a final decision."

"Then why not consider a similar Capital Campaign that encompasses recruitment drives that target more African American students? I mean it is the bases for which the university was founded. Yes, it is no secret that enrollment has been down but why not find ways to get more black bodies in these buildings?"

"Because the diversity avenue provides more opportunities for funding! It takes money to do this education thing right!" I shout frustrated at her resistance. "Let's just face it, Tina! Hardly any HBCUS including ours has ever been able to depend solely on support from alumni to sustain operations. Many of our institutions are suffering tremendously after the cancellations of the football season last year. In this post pandemic era, HBCUS must be even more diligent in securing monies to stay open much less, afloat! We cannot wait on them to do now, what they have never been able to do before!"

"So, more diversity spells more money, huh? What about the history of Heritage? Doesn't that matter anymore?" She spits out to me with much disdain in her voice as she exits the spa haven we had going on before this conversation started. She wraps a towel around her frame and stops in front of the bathroom counter to brush her wet hair."

"Of course, it does but it won't if we can't stay open. I have to consider all options." I protest. "Damn Tina as my wife I need your support on this!"

"Eric, I will never support an initiative to white-wash this school's history. You know why? Because HSU's history is also my family's history, or did you forget about all that?" she issues flatly with the most disgusted look I have seen on her face in a while. As she storms out the bathroom, my mouth is dropped open as I realize, she's probably angrier now than she was when this unexpected tryst first started. *How in the hell did*

I go from Paradise to Isolation in a matter of pure minutes? If this is any indication of how this week is going to unfold, it is truly going to be one long ass week indeed!

Chapter 2
Funny How Life Circles Back
Ananda Harris

"I don't know Dad I have just been feeling unfulfilled lately. It is whack as hell being retired at 36 years old. My entire life has been about the court and now…I don't know what my life is supposed to be about anymore." I confide to my father, Arnold Harris over the phone. Even as a grown ass woman, I have still got to call him and check in whenever I am traveling. The WNBA could not stop that even after I retired. He has always been super proud and over-protective of his one and only. I guess some things never change.

"You have worked extra hard all of your life to achieve your dreams Baby Girl. Believe me, it's okay to not have it all figured out just yet. You only announced your retirement a month after winning your 4th Championship. Give yourself a little time to exhale after a stellar career, Darling."

"I hear you Dad but, I have sacrificed so much for my career and now that it's over, I am beginning to think its past due time for me to redirect my energies. Life is about more than basketball you know." I tell him regretfully.

"You did what you thought was best at the time Ananda. I didn't allow you to beat yourself up about it then and I am not going to allow you to do that now. You have always gone the extra mile to take care of your responsibilities, Honey literally and financially." He reminds me.

"I know but there are still some things that a blank check will not and cannot cover Daddy." I state sternly with finality as I ponder all I gave up for my basketball dreams. *Nowadays, it hardly seems worth it.* I think to myself as I sort through the mail. There are statements to bills paid electronically, a few advertisements and my quarterly copy of the Heritage State Alumni Herald, accompanying a letter from the university addressed to me. The cover image catches me totally off guard, making me drop my toast on the breakfast table.

"Oh my God!" I yell out as I stare at the cover.

"What's wrong Ananda?" My father yells into the phone with urgency in his voice.

"The Heritage State University cover this quarter celebrates the Best of the Best of Alumni and guess who is one of the featured celebs on the cover?" I squeal in excitement.

"My bomb ass daughter that's who!" He cosigns so proudly I can practically hear the smile spreading across his face.

"Yes, well not just of me actually. It's a collage of me with about four other people but still. As many sports' mag covers as I have graced over the years, this one here is mad special Daddy." I say with slight sniffles as I become emotional to be acknowledged this way.

"Of course, it does Baby Girl and you deserve that recognition. That state-of-the-art track you donated to the school and the scholarship program for female athletes you started earned you that cover. Take a pic of it and send it to me asap! I have to put that on my Instagram tonight!" My father demands happily with pride. I still cannot get used to him being active on social media, but Daddy's got to have a life too, I guess.

"We'll do Dad." I say as I open the letter from Heritage. As I read its contents, I can barely hold back my tears. I am so floored that I pinch myself to make sure I am not dreaming. "Oh my God!"

"What's the matter now?" Daddy hollers in another panic.

"The University just selected one of my good friends as the new President and this is a letter announcing my induction into the Heritage State University Sports Hall of Fame! It says here that the ceremony is taking place next month during the Homecoming festivities. They sent me an entire package complete with VIP Passes to the Hall of Fame Banquet, the homecoming game, coronation, alumni breakfast and luncheons, along with a roundtrip ticket, and lodging accommodations." I report solemnly as I remember not having stepped foot on that campus since I left it 18 years ago.

"Wow! That is fantastic Baby Girl! Are you gonna go?"

"I don't know." I say as instant panic makes my stomach quiver. "It's been such a long time."

"Yeah, but a look back may just lead you towards that redirection you said you've been looking for." He says cautiously.

"I know and that's exactly what I am afraid of. I haven't talked with Andre` since the pandemic shut down our travel plans. He's probably pissed the fuck off at me." I say regrettably.

"Maybe, but now would be as good a time as any to fix things with your son, Nanni. It has been time to handle that business." He warns me.

"I know Dad, but what if he rejects me Daddy?"

"Then you keep right on trying until he can't resist. You are his mother Ananda! That does still mean something, Love. But you're never going to know if you don't go."

"I know Dad. I may be scared, but I've still gotta do it. Even if it is the hardest thing, I have ever had to do in my life, it has got to be done." I say aloud to affirm to myself that I am officially on board for the journey to redirection however it comes. Looking at the collage on that cover, only one thing makes me afraid to face my sacrifices. And that's coming face-to-face with my ex-fiancé and son's father, Anthony, also featured in the collage.

He has made quite a name for himself since our breakup as a top personality/producer for Media One and has his own spoken word television series. The invitation mentioned he would be hosting the banquet. TV One will be live streaming the banquet as well as the entire homecoming weekend of events. Seeing my son is icing on the cake in favor of going since he is a junior at Heritage. But seeing his father? Well, that is a recipe for disaster waiting to happen, at the scene of the crime no less. He is going to want answers from me. And I know its way past time he gets them.

Well so be it. *I hear you God and against my better judgment, I obey.*

Chapter 3
Every Woman is Me
Introducing - Destiny Turner

As I do the Honey Stroll with my squad down the center aisles of the auditorium, I am throwing it like a pro. My hips are swaying with each step I take with the precision of a master dancer. I am giving my Janet Jackson walk my best shot, and I can tell by the brothers in the band, that I am killing it to death! As the Captain of the HSU Honey Squad should.

"Work it Destiny!" Our Advisor, and my Auntie, Cierra "Mama Cee-Cee" Folsom cheers me on from the stage. "Yasss Honeys! Work the Walk just like your Captain!" She further encourages from her megaphone.

As the marching band storms in through all the other 4 entrances of the auditorium playing "Danger" by Erykah Badu the vibe is right and the HSU Marching Band is on point! This is the type of rehearsal that gets the band hype right before a performance and this year every performance counts twice as much. This year's homecoming festivities are going to be unprecedented. Our school is one of the first to re-open their campus for a campus wide event since the Corona Virus Pandemic forced the entire HBCU football season, and all conferences to be cancelled last year. Howard University got a stage to grandstand with the 2021 Inauguration of President Joe Biden and Vice President, Kamala Harris, an HU Alum. They were technically the first to open-up their doors, but that was in January. Every other institution has been moving in caution. However, Heritage is in the middle of a transition with a new President in Dr. Eric Smith, and he is hell bent on making history for our school. If his plans work my uncle will put Heritage State University on the map and on the federal government's radar like it has never been before.

It's no surprise though. Everyone I am associated with is a boss. From my parents to my grandparents on both sides, and my aunts and uncles. We are an HSU Clan of sorts and all of us are destined for greatness. My legacy will be no different. It will just be on my own terms as no one is ever going to rule me. I make it a point to keep my nose clean and a firm grip on the upper hand of everything I touch. I get my drive from my mom and dad, Kayla Mansfield-Turner & Cherod Turner and just like with them, when God created me, he outdid himself. As rehearsal wraps up, I notice some loose ends I have got to tie up as well. As everyone is packing to leave, I see someone I need to talk to.

"Hey, EJ! Can I talk to you for a minute?" I inquire sweetly as I throw my bookbag over my shoulder and switch over to the group of drummers he's chatting with.

"Oh yeah sure. Aye I'll holla at yawl later." He issues his goodbyes to his boys and begins walking along beside me out the auditorium and down the hall. "What's up Destiny?"

"What do you mean, what's up Destiny? Don't act like you don't know we've got business!" I whisper as we walk keeping my head held down the entire time.

"I'm not. I was just making conversation. You know I love having business with you." His cute ass teases.

"Quit playing EJ. You know we are not getting down like that anymore! Now focus. First, do you have my meds?" I insist impatiently. *He's always bringing up the fact that we used to mess around. That's some shit I try to forget. Although the sex was bomb, he was too damn clingy for me. Plus, that was back when he was a freshman, and I was a sophomore a million years ago. I know he loved me, but I simply had bigger fish to fry.*

"Yeah, I've got your meds, but you just got a package from me last week. Why do you suddenly need to reup so soon? I mean I know you've got money, but damn girl! What you got going on that's got you smoking weed like a chimney? Mommy and Daddy ain't gonna keep financing your ganja habit if you keep going like that!" His perceptive ass takes way too much notice of my shit.

"Damn you clockin' my chokin', now? Look when you are the Captain of the Honey Squad, a S.T.E.M Major, graduating Senior who is going to be crowned Miss Heritage State University in a few days, you'll know my stress level! Plus, the parents and grandparents are coming down for homecoming too? Hell, it's a wonder how weed is all I do smoke, shit." I chuckle joking with my boy.

Eric Jamal Smith Jr. is more than just a guy I used to date back in the day. He was my friend first. We grew up together as our fathers are frat brothers. His mom and my aunt, Kyla were roommates here at Heritage 20 years ago. We didn't pick each other. Our families were cool. He always had a crush on me and when he beat up a guy for spreading rumors about me in high school, I started seeing him as more than a friend. He was my first everything and I was his too, including his first heartbreak. He was too slow for me once I got here, and by the time he followed me a year later, I was too far gone to take care of him. I used him and hurt him, but he's still been my best friend ever since. They just don't make fellas loyal like EJ anymore.

"So, the Turners the sequel, and the Mansfield's will be here for the coronation huh?" He jokes handing over the thick thesaurus with the pages cut out in the middle where the smelly bag with $100 worth of the finest Kush Sativa inside awaits me. EJ and I have used this method to transport our meds for years. If it ain't broke, why fix it, right?

"And the Original OG Turners too! Shit, both sets of grandparents haven't been together in the same room for a minute so, I'm just making sure I've got enough smoke to make it through the drama." I laugh as I stick the book in my bag. "So, I'll CashApp you the $50 when I get my check Friday."

"Uh, $50? What about the other $50? That's a $100 bag with a little extra I might add. I need all my money, Girl."

"Oh, come on now EJ Baby. I need to get some stuff before the coronation, so I need you to spot me this time, please?" I ask sweetly batting my eye lashes, hoping it works like it has a thousand other times.

"Nawl Girlie. I need my ends. Unless…you're offering another way to pay off this debt?" He leads me with the sexiest smile. *Damn he is still fine as fuck.* I know where this going.

"Another way to pay? What does your nasty ass have in mind EJ?"

"You know how we play Destiny." He growls at me stepping up to whisper that shit in my ear. My panties instantly moisten.

"Well, it would be a shame if your parents found out how you have been peddling ganja that you have growing in the basement of the boarded-up Ellington Hall all up and through this campus and Fitzwater's for all the years you've been here. That's how I'm playing."

"You wouldn't! How the hell you gone threaten me with snitching when you are one of my biggest customers?"

"Look Lil Nino, when you start trying to get me to play for pay, the kid gloves come off and shit gets hella real. So, what do you say EJ? I will continue to keep my mouth shut if you let that little $50 go. If we have a deal, then you might still get a date. I mean after all we have always played well together." I flirt as I lay down my bottom line. Yes, I could get the money from my parents with no problems, but I am an independent woman. I like to get it where I live, even if it is sometimes in the gutter.

"Indeed, we do Destiny, have a deal that is for now anyway. Look I've gotta jet but, I'ma be looking to cash in on that date real soon Miss Heritage. And you know you're wrong for even joking about telling my peeps what you think you know. That shit ain't even funny." He warns me with that sexy grin once again.

"I wasn't trying to be funny Homie. And I don't see nothing wrong with using a little leverage my brother. You know that. Plus, as long as your bottom line is met does it really matter EJ?"

"Yeah, it does matter to me, especially when it comes to you." He admits. *He couldn't stop it if he tried.* I think to myself as he continues. "But I see you so now I know and knowing is half the battle, right?"

"Right." I offer indifferently as we part ways and I make my way back to my apartment with a guilt-free conscience to prep for my next meeting. Blackmailing my friend to get a discount on some smoke is nothing. This homecoming is going to be epic for me and that means I am going to have to call in a lot of favors. I've got a wish list that must be fulfilled, and it will too, by any means necessary!

Chapter 4
As the Band Sings the Blues
Dr. DeJuan Dexter
HSU Marching & Concert Band Director
HSU Class of 2004

As band rehearsal in Louis Armstrong auditorium ends, seeing my best friend and Dean of the College of Fine & Performing Arts, Dr. Chavon Turner headed my way makes me nervous and happy at the same time. See happy I am always when I get time to kick back with my friend. We did undergrad and grad school here together, and fun is an under description of our time hanging out. But nowadays our schedules clash here like you would not believe. We may work in the same department, but we have different interests and responsibilities. Plus, our personal lives keep us busy too, so we haven't chilled like homeboys in months. That's what's got me nervous. The look of sheer stress on his face lets me know he's not coming to set up a cigar date for the fellas. Once virtually all the left-over students are gone. He states his business.

"What's going on Bruh? Fancy seeing you over in these parts." I tease him as we dap up and he plops down next to me on the edge of the stage.

"Well, you know if I'm around these parts its serious, right?" Chavon alerts me, staring me dead in the eyes over his Gucci glasses. *This nigga is still such a damn diva.* I laugh to myself.

"Alright Bro hit me with it." I lead taking off my glasses and meeting his stare down head on. Now he should know by now that I do not intimidate easily. I am aware my boy has got a job to do, but shit, so do I.

"Well, Juan my dude, I couldn't get the Board to approve your budget amounts for the year. They said you are going to have to go back to the drawing board and come down another $20,000." He finishes regrettably.

The steam forming around my neck is making the hair in my fade curl as I instantly get heated. It's taking all I have to keep my cool before responding. "Go back to the drawing board? I'm a goddamn musician, not magician! How in the hell can yawl expect me to run the caliber of program this school runs for twenty grand less than last year's budget? You have got to be fucking kidding me right now?" I snap. So much for keeping my cool. But what can I say? A brother is passionate.

"Juan, man it is not me! If it were up to me brother, you would have all you need, no matter the cost. But shit just doesn't work like that man. What do you want me to say?" He quizzes with a look on his that begs me to look at the situation from his point of view. And I will as soon as he sees it from mines.

"What do I want you to say? Are you serious? I want you to tell the damn Board that your award-winning marching and concert bands have been rocking the same tired ass uniforms for the last ten years! I want you to let them know we are in dire need of new instruments as many we have now are not working. Oh, and then tell them how they are fucking killing my recruitment by cutting the scholarships for my auxiliary! Chavon, that's my Majorettes, Flags & the Honey Squad! I want you to tell them that less scholarship dollars equals loss of great students! I'm talking the kind of kids skilled enough to write and compose music for this program! Tell them we are already losing students in droves and the music department is one of its most sought- after programs! That's what I want you to say! Da fuck do you mean?" I say to him fire-breathing dragon mad at this point. Two light skinned brothers intellectually arguing valid points with fire is surely a sight to see, I am sure. That's why I'm glad no one else is here right now.

"And then what Juan? What do I do when I have said everything you mentioned and more and they still say, *no, go back and tell him this!* Brother please don't tell me that you don't think I fight for you!" He offers in disappointment, calming his tone a bit.

"Well, that's sure not what it feels like when you come to me with shit like this." I counter.

"I feel that but look, I didn't just come up in here with bad news. I've got some ideas about how to get some outside funding for your program and the kids, separate from the rest of the department. I mean these ideas are not guarantees though Juan. They are longshots but, I believe in our program and its leader."

My homie leads as a slick grin comes across his face and I can swear I see his mind spinning as we speak.

"Bout fucking time! What have you got in mind?"

"Well, there's the Big Midwest Battle of the Bands, the Big Southern Challenge and the Sprite Battle of the Bands. I think HSU should enter them all. You all are more than qualified." Chavon preaches to me like I don't already know my band is the shit.

"Yeah, I hear that, but those contests have hefty entry fees, travel/lodging and meal expenses and all that requires funding my brother." I remind him.

"Not this year!" He quickly reminds me. "Due to the pandemic, submissions and the Finals will be live streamed from the participating schools individually, and with voting at the end. That means no travel, meal, and lodging costs."

"Damn the budget usually only allows for us to enter one of those contests a year. It's usually so damn costly."

"Right, so now we can afford to enter HSU in all three. But ah…that will probably take a big chunk out of the budget. What are you all willing to do on your end? If I am not doing enough, help me out a little damn!" Chavon yells.

"Okay finally you're walking over to my side of this thing. Now that I've got your fucking attention here's what I am going to need you to do for me." I offer for him to sit back down, and I do the same as we both had made it back to our feet in the heat of the moment. "Create enough wiggle room for us to host some independent fund raisers. I mean nothing we have to split with any other entity because other than the stuff I mentioned earlier, we still have other expenses and the loss of traveling gigs for last year's season damn near killed our program. But…I think we can raise a great deal between now and then if you can keep administration off my fucking back."

"You know I will do whatever I can to help Juan. We were in Heritage's band together many moons ago Dog. I know what you need and believe it or not I am on your side in this battle man."

"I know Chavon, but I've got to be real about the situation. You have got to look out for the entire department. But my job, is all about this band and its students, man. I will always go hard for them."

"And that's why you're here, man. I got your back but move cautiously and quietly my brother. Cover your ass, so that I do not have to. You feel me?" He warns me as he stands to leave, and we dap up again.

"Alright man. We still on for dinner over your house tonight? What's Kyla cooking?" I ask killing this heavy ass conversation for now.

"Yeah man, and she's got corned beef, cabbage, macaroni and cheese and hot water cornbread on deck." He says excitedly as he heads back up the aisle the way he came in.

"Awl, hell yeah! What time should I be there?" I ask as my stomach growls.

"The usual time Dog, 7 o'clock. See you then." He smiles as he leaves.

"You damn right Chavon. I will see you and raise your efforts too if I have to." I say inwardly before heading out myself.

Chapter 5
Life is but a Dream
Introducing – Dream Latrice Turner

"Dream will you please hurry your ass up! I don't have time to be on your 20-minute morning shower shit today! I've got an 8 o'clock class!" My suitemate, Tamia hollers from the other side of our bathroom door. I am so glad enrollment is down because that afforded us the opportunity to have single rooms. But we still share a bathroom and that's what's got this cow yelling at the top of her lungs this morning rushing me.

"Oh alright! Pull your panties out your ass, here I come, damn!" I announce with much attitude as I strut my petite behind out the bathroom without a care in the world.

"Thank you, Queen Dream for bringing your slow, privileged ass out the shitter finally!" She barks angrily.

"Don't start with me this morning Tamia! Your ass has been up since 5 am for band practice! Why you waited until after seven to get ready for an 8 am class is beyond me!" I huff right back to her in frustration. Shit I am not used to punching no damn time clock for other people. At home I don't have to share. I'm the only one there.

"I just got back from band practice for your information. And since your privileged ass usually doesn't turn over til ten, I thought I'd be able to catch a quick shower. That way I won't have to go to class funky as fuck! Anyway, what's got you up and at it so early this morning?"

"Well, if you must know. I am going to the am clinics for the Honey Auditions." I tell her waiting for some snide remark from my hater ass suitemate. Although Tamia is a gorgeous Gabrielle Union flava brown girl, her tongue is often lethal. She's a nut that's a lot of fun when she's not stressed out but, its marching band season so...*I see the Diva is on duty!* I laugh to myself. "Girl after yesterday's rehearsal I need all the help I can get if I'm want to make the squad." I explain with less attitude and more excitement.

"So, you decided to try out huh? I thought you didn't like all the attention the Honey

Squad gets. You said you didn't need that kind of attention." She challenges me in a cynical tone now conversating with me through the closed bathroom door.

"Well, that was then, and this is now! I think I've really got a shot. But I know with my suitemate's veteran Honey help I will be a virtual shoe in!" I suggest batting my lashes and smiling extra hard even though she can't see me.

"Sure, I'll help you out but there might not even be a damn Honey Squad soon."

"What are you talking about Tamia?" I ask her with the duck lips.

"I heard the school is cutting the band's budget and scholarships. If it's true, then we are going to lose a lot of members. And who do you think they are coming for first, the Flags, Majorettes and Honey Squad. All bullshit aside, it looks like our dancing days just may be numbered Dream."

"Damn, my mom didn't say anything about all this to me when I talked to her about it this morning. She just told me that it would be good for me to try something outside of my comfort zone." I say perplexed as to why she neglected to let me know the band program is in trouble like that. *I mean after all she is on the damn HSU Board of Trustees, so I know she knows.* I think.

"Look I'm not telling you to not go for it. Just don't be surprised if and when the bottom drops out. That's all I'm saying. But I'll help you if you want me to Dream. I may give you a hard time but, you are still my girl." Tamia smiles at me hard coming out the bathroom. "Just get ready for the other part of being a Honey if you make it." She warns me heading over to her room. After hearing that, I march right up behind her.

"What do mean the other part of being a Honey? Because I already know the practices are hard and learning different routines every week takes a different kind of discipline. So, what are you referring to?" I ask staring Tamia down like I'm her judge and jury. If she is really my girl like she just professed to be, then she better spill the tea.

"I just mean some of the old heads like to initiate the newbies. If you know what I mean." She leads me with a side eye as she settles at her desk where her laptop is open, about to log on for class. Everything here is virtual these days thanks to the Corona Virus.

"Oh that, girl have you met my family? I was raised on that shit! That's why I ain't sweating it now! My Mom, my aunt and my grandparents are Greek! Pledging was a part of my rearing!" I joke as we both break up laughing.

Just as I finish that sentence, we hear a knock at my door. Before either of us can ask, who the hell is it, in saunters my overbearing, overprotective and over-the-top first and only cousin, Destiny from my side of the suite. Her movement is fluid through the space as if she lives here and her mouth is running so fast, barking orders that she is oblivious to what either of us might have going on in our own fucking room. *Unbelievable!* We just watch her breeze her curvy-slim ass through our space like she owns the place in awe at the audacity of her.

"Dreamy Bear Girl, I am so glad I found you! I've got so many things that must get done before this coronation and I need my favorite sister/cousin's help. I've got to go shopping for shoes and accessories, I've still got to see who is going to do my make-up that evening…blah blah blah" she rambles on without even saying hello. Typical Destiny.

"First of all, I am your only sister/cousin so being your favorite is a non-fucking factor, so miss me with that mess. Second, you are the one being crowned Miss Heritage State not me!" I say full of sarcasm just to fuck with my cousin. I love to do it because it is so easy to get under her skin. I really do love her like a big sister, and I am going to help her even if I don't feel like it. If it means something to her then it means something to me.

"And I can't do that without your help Cuzzie! So, stop tripping and let's go fire up the Cruz!" She barks at me like I work for her.

"Hell no! Your errands need to be ran in your fucking car! Not mines!" I resist.

"My Escape is in the shop! I should be getting it back later this afternoon, so I just got dropped off over here. Come on Dream quit playing I've got shit to do." She urges me like she's running out of patience. *Unbelievable times two!*

I march passed Destiny back into my room, grab my purse and pull my cars keys out. When I toss them in my cousin's direction my suitemate busts up laughing as Destiny catches the keys like we rehearsed it even though it visibly startles her.

"Here you can use my car, but I am going to the Honey AM Clinic this morning! Sorry." I say indifferently but my cousin ain't having it.

"The Clinics? Girl bye! They cancelled today's clinic last night for an emergency meeting with the Board this morning. Plus, since when do you want to be on the Honey Squad, Dream?" She asks like the thought is preposterous and that grinds my gears.

"Ah don't act like you're the only talented one in the family Destiny! I took dance right next to you for 12 years! I've got skills too, okay?"

I defend adamantly. Truth be told, I'm sweeter than Destiny and she knows it.

"I didn't even say that Dream! You could make the squad with no problem, but what about your other responsibilities? Our practice schedule is intense, and won't it interfere with your HSU Ambassador work and the modeling troop? Girl you can't be everywhere at once." She reminds me.

I hadn't really thought about all that. The modeling troop decided to hold a few shows virtually as a fundraiser at our last meeting. Plus, the ambassadors have got us doing virtual meetings with our freshmen groups weekly. As much as I hate to admit it, Destiny might have a valid point here.

"Plus, with the money gossip all over campus, the band might not have a fucking Honey Squad. You better let those sweet dreams just fly away, honey!" Destiny jokes poking much fun at my expense. Tamia is snickering too. *Did I mention I hate it when she's right? Damn.*

"Damn Destiny! You really know how to wreck the energy in the room, you know that?" I profess totally defeated and disappointed.

"Girl please I am just keeping it 100 so you won't waste your precious time. Now are you coming with me or not?" She urges once again, back to things being all about her.

"Fuck it. I might as well go. You coming, Tamia?" I ask as I direct my attention back to Tamia to irk Destiny since she has yet to even acknowledge Tamia's presence. She just paraded in on her own brand of bullshit considering no one else but herself, as usual.

"Nawl Dream I've got work to do here so I'ma just talk to yawl later." Tamia offers modestly, all-of-a-sudden as she turns to leave the room. Five minutes ago, she was all fiery and once Destiny came in Tamia's fire went out. As she passes her, Destiny finally speaks up.

"Oh, and Tamia don't forget about the mandatory Honey Meeting at my apartment this evening. It starts at 7 pm sharp." Destiny orders.

"I'll be there, Destiny." Tamia replies indifferently before leaving and shutting her door. Once she is gone, Destiny goes right back to Diva shit."

"Well come on. I've got to get these errands done before I have to be at the Dean of Students office at Fitzwater."

"What time do you have to be there?" I ask grabbing up my purse again.

"At one o'clock, then I've got be back home by five to watch Baby Jaylyn so Jazzmen can get to work and get ready for that meeting at seven. It's gonna be a long day."

"How did you get a work study job over at Fitzwater? You don't even go to school there Cuz." I ask curiously staring at her like a catholic school nun. Why? Because my dear, sweet cousin is always working some sort of angle. Please believe me.

"It's not a work study job. I'm on the school's payroll. It's only part time but hey every little bit helps, right? Plus, you know a sistah's got gifts and expenses, right?" She brags as a somewhat sinister smile creeps across my cousin's face.

"Your ass is always working up on something, aren't you Destiny?"

"Don't be mad at me because I make my work, work for me, Dream. Now come on. Let's go." She issues sternly as she sashays out the dorm with my obedient ass following up right behind her.

Chapter 6
Same House, Different Sides
Jacqueline Mansfield

"Look, I understand that we are in the midst of a budget crunch but pursuing multi-cultural status disqualifies us for land grant institution funding and that should most certainly be out of the question." I defend at the emergency Board meeting. We are all assembled with the National Alumni Association officers, the new President of Heritage, Eric Smith and of course all my colleagues on the HSU Board of trustees, including my husband of almost 30 years, Michael Mansfield.

"Multi-cultural status would open up Heritage to a barrage of funding opportunities on the federal level not readily available to black colleges." My husband advises cautiously, looking in the opposite direction of me because he knows his opposition puts him on my shit list.

"That's when we have to enlist our alumni to make up the difference. They have been coming through in droves for various scholarship efforts during the government shut down. Maybe now is the time to re-direct that energy." My youngest daughter, Kyla's friend and wife of the new president, Tina Hutchins-Smith suggests.

"Now when have you ever heard of any HBCU surviving solely on the strength of its alumni?" Michael poses sarcastically.

"I haven't but that means now is as good a time as any for change, don't you think?" Tina replies with the quick wit I've come to love about her. She keeps it real and I, for one, can respect and appreciate that.

"Well arguing for another couple hours about this, is not going to solve anything! Its 48 hours until the Hall of Fame Banquet and Homecoming 2021 kick-off and at the annual general alumni meeting, people are going to expect a decision to have been made and a plan put into action to financially sustain this school. We need to decide which method of funding we're going to pursue. What do you think Dr. Smith?" One of the elder Trustees asks Eric.

As he sits among us at the head of the long oak wood meeting table with reps from the Board of Trustees in support of multi-cultural funding plans and National Alumni Association members prepared to settle in for a long hard fight to uphold our land-grant institution status that preserves our traditional HBCU funding opportunities on either side of the table, one can see the stress on his brow. He has the hardest of decisions to make and there are no guarantees with either. Only folks to disappoint. I do not envy him in the slightest.

"Well, brothers and sisters you have all made compelling arguments and the proposals submitted representing both campaigns are organized, well-thought out and offer substantial potential for our school. Being the member that holds the deciding vote to break our gridlock on this issue, I have made a very, difficult decision." He begins as the room goes deafly silent. He has everyone's full attention. "Instead of choosing one campaign over the other, when all proposals offer compelling and exciting opportunities in their own right, I have decided I will not choose." As soon as the final syllable escapes Dr.

Smith's mouth, the collective gasps take over as the shock becomes visible on every face, including that of his wife, Tina.

She knew that her husband had been conflicted however, deep down in her heart of hearts, she still must have believed he would side with her. Although I thought the same way before this very moment, I find myself even more intrigued to discover his rationale for the decision.

"What exactly do you mean when you say, you will not choose President Smith?" My husband, Michael asks before I can get the words out.

"I mean that since both campaigns offer solutions we should actively and aggressively pursue both. After all, I see no problem with each committee going forth with their plans. In my opinion we can never have too many fundraising efforts going on as there is always something needing financial support at an HBCU. Heritage State is no different." He explains.

"You cannot be serious!" One board member boosts in opposition. "That is preposterous! You have got to decide! It's your damn job!"

"With all due respect, I believe I just announced my decision and although you may not agree with it, I am very much doing my damn job, Sir. Heritage can benefit from both campaigns, and we obviously have enough people in favor of both to get it all done. I see no reason to abandon one for the other. Now since the tie breaking vote lies with me, if there are no other objections, by a show of hands, all in favor say, I." Eric holds his position firmly and professionally as he scans the room of hands that go up, a few of which were previously on either side of the coin. "By a show of hands, all those opposed say Ney." There are more hands totaling in favor of the joint campaigns and the meeting continues with other issues, and committee selections.

I am surprisingly, impressed with the way Dr. Eric Smith handled the business of both the Trustees and the Alumni. They can be intimidating to say the least to a seasoned veteran so watching his youthful, albeit grown man self in action was entertaining and educational at the same time. I am looking forward to these homecoming festivities because our new president will not be bullied, nor moved on anyone else's agenda. Now, that probably doesn't sit too well with my husband because Michael Mansfield just loves to throw his weight around, but it looks like *it's a new day, and that is a damn good thing for Heritage State.* I think to myself as the meeting concludes with side-eyes and shitty faces all over the room because everyone and no one got their way today.

Chapter 7
Living on a Wing and a Prayer
Cierra Folsom

I am stumbling through the parking lot of Wine & Wings, a quaint, little neat pub about 5 minutes from the campus. It's not fancy but they have the best wings and drinks one can find in this hick-ass town, and I am famished beyond belief after that meeting with Juan. My mind is spinning a million miles a minute, after being ambushed with the news of more budget cuts aimed at my program on the fucking horizon. Juan is the damn Band Director, so I know he is just as upset as I am but, this shit is not right. It has been out of hand. We are already struggling making miracles happen on a streamlined budget and have been for the last 10 years.

I have got to find a way to stop the fucking bleeding financially or its gonna be a wrap for the whole HSU Marching Band Auxiliary as we have always known it. *As the Coordinator for the last 21 years, I cannot let that happen, not on my watch. No fucking way!* I think to myself as I damn near fall through the swinging glass door of the establishment. I need a meal and a stiff drink to think in the worst way. As soon as I get settled at the bar and get my wing meal and cranberry Cosmo ordered, my cell phone lights up with a sho-nuff blast from my past on the line that instantly makes my day as I anxiously answer.

"Hey Tina! What's wrong?" I ask suspiciously of my homegirl.

"Hey, why does something have to be wrong? Can't I just call my Sis to catch up?" She asks on the defensive. That's my first clue something's up.

"Not when we're supposed to be meeting up at Kyla and Chavon's tonight for dinner, no. So again, I ask what's wrong?" I insist.

"Girl I just got out of that fucking board meeting and Eric just flipped the script on everyone! I must admit he made a ballsy move that I didn't even see coming! I just knew he was gonna lean my way with the rest of the alumni to preserve our land grant, historically black status and..."

"You mean he went with the Trustees in favor of multi-cultural means instead?" I almost yell through the phone in disbelief.

"No, no, no…he decided that both campaigns can actively proceed with their efforts. He didn't choose. He challenged each side to do what they could. He gave both entities the go ahead to pursue their submitted campaigns and thus make the university be the benefactor." She explains.

"That's sounds like a bomb plan Tina so why are you trippin? He didn't reject your side."

"Yeah, but he didn't choose my side either, Cee-Cee. This school is tied to my family lineage. How can I support any campaign that looks to erase that?"

"Sis you don't have to support that campaign. Your job is to support Eric, your husband, you know that guy you had two beautiful babies by that just so happens to be the new president of the school we all graduated from? He is under enough pressure without you making this a point of contention between the two of you don't you think?" I warn her because she needs to hear this.

"I hate it when you're right you know that?" She relents with a huge sigh.

"Yes, I know." I giggle, nodding thanks to the waitress that brings my food and drink.

"Okay I had to get that out before my next class. I'll see you tonight at the Turners?"

"Yep, I'll be there. Are you sure you're good now?"

"Yeah, I'm good. You're right, Eric needs my support, not another battle. I heard you." She issues sadly.

"That's right now go teach those monsters how to be great in English Lit Professor Hutchins-Smith and I will see you later." I demand jokingly before we disconnect the call and I prepare to smash these wings and fries.

In all my excitement about eating I drop my fork. That's when it happens. I start to bend down to get the fork and bump foreheads hard as fuck with the most gorgeous black man I have seen in a good long time.

Clunk! Echoes in the room first and we both pop back up to the sitting position on our respective stools, looking stupid as hell, like twin crash dummies after the trauma. Rubbing my forehead, I can't help but laugh a little when I see him rubbing his too. He's a mocha chocolate, bearded beautiful man with a short wavy fade, pearly white teeth and hazel eyes. He's got the kind of eyes that, looking into them, fucks up your vision, and you can't see straight much less, think of a thing to say. Yes ladies, he is that fine.

"Ouch!" I offer for lack of anything better.

"Ditto." He laughs as he hands me my fork.

"Thank you. I am so sorry for damn near knocking you off your stool." I lead with a slight smile as I fold the fork up into my napkin. When the waitress comes over to bring me another fork, he takes it from her and hands it to me with a huge smile. I smile back and feel a sensation go through me that I haven't entertained in years. It's kind of shocking but it feels good too.

"No need to apologize. A good hot plate of crispy wings can get folks excited like that sometimes." He jokes and I'm relieved he doesn't seem to notice he's turning me on just by talking to me.

"Oh yes, and these are the best. I have been thinking about this plate all morning and after the meeting I just came from, I need some comfort food." I confess like he asked for all that info. I instantly start to turn red. He laughs again and it makes me feel better.

"Well hell since you're bragging on them like that, maybe I should order up a plate myself. That is if you don't mind a little company." He offers smoothly. I thought he might be flirting since we are still talking and all, but now I'm sure he's flirting, and I think I like it.

"No, I don't mind. After all it's the least I can do after damn near giving you a concussion a minute ago." I joke with a smile.

"Cool," he states scooting over to the empty stool right next to me. "So now that we are officially on our first lunch date, who do I have the pleasure of dining with for lunch today?" He asks suavely staring me dead in my eyes.

"Oh wow. Is that what this is? And more importantly, how many random women do you pick up at bars with good wings a week, Sir?"

"In this town? Just one, and she indeed best believe this is a date. Our first for now but it won't be our last." He says seriously without cracking a smile.

"Oh really?"

"Yes really! Now who do I have the pleasure of dining with?" He persists.

"I don't know what you take me for, but I do not just go around handing my name, rank and serial number out to good looking strangers all willy-nilly. I don't know you from Adam." I insist.

"Well, since you think I'm good looking, fuck it. Let's start from the beginning then. Hello beautiful lady I'm about to lick my fingers in front of you eating these wings. My name for now is Adam X." He announces with a wide smile. "Now you officially know me from Adam, and I'll just call you Eve. How about that?" He insists as his food is placed in front of him. I think it over for about a millisecond and relent with the quickness. I mean after all, he is too fine.

"Fuck it. Okay Eve it is. Pleasure to meet you, Adam." I cave shaking his hand and proceeding to handle the business at hand of smashing my food.

Over the next hour Adam and I talk about the food of course, where we went to college, and the area since he's new to it. The more we conversate, the more fun I find myself having. I mean we are joking and vibing like we have been friends for years, and we don't even know the other's real name. That fact alone is so sexy to me that it intrigues the shit out of me. The more intrigued I become however, that familiar fear starts to set in, and it scares the shit out of me more than my intrigue.

That's when I know I've got to cut this thing short right now.

"You know this has all been a great time, but I need to get back to work." I state in a rush wiping my hands and clearing up the mess around me, in efforts to not give him eye contact.

"Oh, ah okay then sure I understand that. But um it's been so much fun chilling with you Eve…" he says sincerely before grabbing my hands up into his to stop my cleaning to look at him. "I don't want the fun to stop. Can I call you and maybe take you out on a real date?"

"I don't think so Adam. This was fun and all. Don't get me wrong, but I am not dating right now." I stutter with my head down.

"Oh well if you don't mind me asking, why is a woman as fine as you not dating? Who stole your joy, Lady?"

"No one I am just not dating at the moment, okay?" I state flatly in irritation now.

"Okay, but I think that's mad unfortunate!" He insists.

"Maybe so, but that's the way it is you know? Sorry, but I've got to go." I grab up my check from the bar and he promptly snatches it out of my hand.

"I've got that. You can at least let me buy you lunch since I am obviously making you late getting back to work, okay?"

"Okay fine, thanks and it was really nice kind of meeting you." I extend before grabbing up my purse.

"Prove it. Put your name and number in my phone." He suggests with a sly grin now. This man is relentless.

"What?"

"You heard me. If it was so nice meeting me, give me your number in case I get lost or something. I told you I'm new in town."

"So, google maps ain't good enough for you, huh?" I inquire sarcastically as I take his phone and enter my digits under the name EVE into his contacts and hand it back to him. He calls me right there on the spot and smiles.

"Lock me in as ADAM and I'll talk to you soon EVE! He sings as we both listen to my phone ringing as I make my way out the door.

I can't deny how good it feels to have a man that damn handsome shoot his shot with me. But I am not the one. Love ain't lived here in a long ass time and I ain't about to get into no lust life type shit now. The single life is my best life indeed. I ponder inwardly as I make my way to my car, trying to get that fine ass man off my fucking mind.

Chapter 8
When Business Becomes Personal
Destiny Turner

When I finally make it back to my apartment after running all over town with Dream, and my part-time gig and Fitzwater, I am pleased to see that most of the Honey Squad has already made it there for the meeting. We're just waiting on a few of the Flags and Majorettes to get here so we can get started. It is mandatory so those that do not make it will have hell to pay. I don't call meetings after hours often, so everyone needs to take this very seriously. And those who don't will definitely miss out. Once the others finally arrive, I finally get down to business.

"Okay ladies I called this after-hours meeting to put you all up on game. This year's Auxiliary budget is being reduced drastically and unless we come up with fundraising efforts to supplement the missing dollars, we will not have a season this year." I explain seriously.

"Well why are they cutting our budget so much?" Tamia, Dream's roommate yells out with attitude.

"It's not just Us. They are cutting the budget for the entire band. When they get cuts, we get cuts. Now Dr. Dexter is already working on fundraising strategies, but I feel like we need to be looking out for ourselves. Many of you are Seniors and intended to end this year with a bang. The rest of you need to help us so you can have something to begin with next season, or at least know how to get it back if this funding trend continues."

"That shit sucks." One of the flag girls protests.

"Yes, it does, but I say let's brainstorm solutions rather than bitch and moan about the problem." Brittney, my Co-Captain maintains, and the ideas start flowing.

"How about a bake & candy sale series?" Kendra, the Flag Captain suggests.

"Ut uh, I am not trying to be dealing candy and cookies for no fucking chump change.

We can do better than that, ladies come on."
Sarah, the Diva Majorette shoots down with
her nose turned all the way up.

"How about we get it how we live." Mariah,
the head diva Majorette leads the group.

"What's that supposed to mean Mariah?"
Brittney asks with much sarcasm.

"It means use what we've got to get what we
want. Sex sells on this campus, and no one is
sexier on this yard than us. So, why not
capitalize on that shit and do a calendar? The
men on this campus will eat that shit up.
Think about it 12 sexy, yet tasteful pictures
featuring the HSU Majorettes, Flag Core &
Honey Squad will sell around this bitch like
hot cakes." Mariah boosts and every girl in the
room agrees.

"I like that idea." Tamia agrees cheesing from
ear to ear.

"Hell, me too. I like it even better than my
ideas." Sarah confesses seriously.

"Well unless anyone else has another idea, let's bring this one to a vote." I encourage to keep the girls on track as I have other business that needs to be addressed with some of these ladies. "All those in favor of the calendar raise your hand." When I see the unanimous gesture it's a wrap. "Well, alrighty then, a calendar it is!" I announce as the girls all clap in agreement.

We continue the meeting by working out the particulars of the calendar like shoot ideas, timeline for completion, and distribution. We made sure the majorettes, flags and honeys get 2 group shots each, 6 full auxiliary shots (3 poses and 3 action) that will provide the 12 photos needed to produce a high-quality 2022 HSU Auxiliary Calendar. Promotion will start right after Thanksgiving and sales start right before the end of the semester. Once we go over the week's rehearsal schedule for homecoming week, and uniform checks it is time to adjourn this meeting.

"Well Ladies, it looks like we have covered most everything on the agenda so, I call this meeting a wrap, but seniors for each group, I need you all to stay a little longer to go over particulars for this week if you don't mind." I issue kindly as the ladies begin to pack up to leave. Once the rest of the ladies are gone, it is time to get down to the real business for tonight's meeting.

"Okay Ladies, I am going to get straight to the point. I know you guys always hear about money troubles all the time with this school, but this cut is gonna hurt our program the most." I explain to the six ladies still here, Honey Co and Assistant Captains Brittany & Tamia, Majorette Captains-Sarah & Mariah, Kennedy, Drew and Imani from the Flag Core.

"Well how is it that you know so much about what all the higher ups have been trying to keep secret?" Kennedy speaks up with much sarcasm.

"Let's just say I have my ways. Anyway, for most of our squads, the crunch won't stop them from being in school. Mommy and Daddy will just pick up the slack on their tuition balances. However, for many of you all, the solution is not that easy as you all get the biggest scholarship dollars for your part on these squads. When the crunch comes down, your money is going to disappear and I know that's a hit most of you can't afford to take, right," I explain then inquire with what I hope comes off as compassion?

"Yeah, so what's your point, Destiny?" Imani rushes me and I am instantly reminded why I can't stand her bitch ass. She is a total snot.

"My point, Imani is that I have a proposition of sorts to help possibly supplement those funds for you ladies. I mean if you're interested." I lead the group and seeing the intrigue on their faces, I go on. "There are several events planned this week to cater to our visiting, older alums that will be traveling from far and wide for homecoming."

"So…" Imani interrupts and resisting the urge to dot her eye, I smack my lips, toss my hair over my shoulder to dismiss her ass and continue.

"So…that means there is sure to be a bevy of older folks looking for something to do after the events and maybe even someone to do it with, if you all get my drift."

"Are you suggesting we be their tour guides or something like that?" Mariah's Pollyanna ass asks like she's smells a rat.

"No not tour guides per-say, more like escorts of sorts. Companions to keep them happy and entertained during their visit. The happier alumni are, the more money they spend."

"Girl I know you're not suggesting what I think you're suggesting!" Sarah yells out with enough disdain in her voice to choke a camel. *I've gotta get this bitch together real quick.*

"I am suggesting a means to you all lining your purses with a little profit over empty ass promises. If you've got a better suggestion Sarah, please enlighten us. But if not sit down and shut the fuck up." I start politely enough but finish through gritted teeth.

"Look, I am all about my paper. I don't know about yawl, but I am too fucking close to finally finishing to let money hold me up now. Destiny, tell us more shit." Drew explains seriously and all the other ladies tune in.

"Well yawl know my parents are on the Board of Trustees so many of these older alums I have known since I was a kid. I know how they work. I have created this membership only, private, paid website called The Urban Upscale Experience where folks can find short term companions. Once I add photos of the girls willing to participate, members will be able to book time with you through me. They submit their date requirements and I review submissions and match you all up. You set the price with the agreement I get 25% and the dates are booked. Funds are secured before the date and your money is deposited to your accounts through CashApp within an hour of the date's end. Services start at $500 ladies." I explain.

"So basically, you're trying to pimp us, right Destiny?" Imani announces like she's the moral majority in the room.

"Call it what you want Imani, but you've been passing out pussy for props since I've known your ass. Don't you think it's about time you pop that passed-around pussy for a purpose?"

As I finish my statement my cell phone buzzes in my pocket. I check the number and see my alumni connect is trying to contact me. I step into the hallway to take the call.

Upon returning to the living room, the girls are all still discussing my offer. So, there is no time like the present to see what they all have to say.

"Well ladies, are we doing business together this week or nah?" I pose pleasantly knowing not many of them have any other options.

"I am not trying to be caught with no old farts during homecoming." Kennedy exclaims with her nose turned up.

"Please, Kennedy your biggest concern should be convincing me to not tell your roommate you're fucking her father and have been since he dropped her off last semester, every time she turns her back. Old farts are your fucking specialty, bitch and we all know it. So, miss me with the charade." I spit out cruelly without hesitation. "And Imani please let us not forget the low-post-player behavior you displayed all summer dancing at the local strip club trying to twerk up on tuition. You ain't slick bitch, we saw you!" I whisper sarcastically with a sinister smirk.

"Damn Destiny, you're calling sisters out like that?" Imani yells.

"Hell, yeah I'm calling yawl ass out! I am not about to stand here with yawl looking down your noses at me when most of yawl's hoe-escapades are legend! Last time I looked I ain't see anybody else handing out solutions or checks, so what's it gonna be? At least I'm offering options to keep yawl here!" I offer sardonically, but seriously all the same. I'm more than a little offended that some of these bitches tried to act appalled. *Fuck they think this is?*

"Well, ahh I know this is a strange way to end this meeting, but a lot has to be considered and I don't think it would be fair to expect any of you to make a decision tonight. So, think it over, but she'll need answers by tomorrow after Noon at the latest." Jazmeen hurries to clear the air of all the thick ass tension and adjourn the meeting. *My girl, she always has my back.*

The ladies pack up and leave and Jaz sees them out one by one as I sit stewing over in the corner of the living room. Once they're all gone, she comes over and sits next to me.

"These bitches get on my last nerve Sands, acting like they don't need that money." I hiss still mad as hell.

"I know Sands, but those hoes will come around. They may not admit it in front of the crowd but, they'll get with you. Watch what I say. You know I'm down; I've got a son to feed so you already know." She explains.

"Cool, but I'ma need your tech expertise on this project to keep our noses clean. Let the minions do the dirty work, and you and I can handle the real big girl business, making sure none of this shit can be traced back to us, deal?" I offer.

"Deal Sands…you, me and the coin makes three!" She exclaims as we hug and suddenly, I feel better about our options in this money game to save our season, by the oldest means available indeed.

Chapter 9
Dealing with the Details over Dinner
The Turners & Friends

Kyla

Here I am in the kitchen putting the finishing touches on tonight's meal by myself, as usual. Where is my husband you ask? Laid out on the couch funking up my damn living room right before his company is scheduled to arrive. *Typical.* I say scheduled because for the last two years, his boy, okay our boy, Juan has joined us for dinner every Monday night without fail. I don't care if it's a hurricane, if it's on a Monday Juan is taking cover with us weather invited or not. My ungrateful, unappreciative husband of too many goddamn years, Chavon could at least help a sister out a little by showering and getting his stinky clothes downstairs to the laundry room in our basement. But no, not my husband. Instead, he just gives me more to do with his selfish ass behavior.

"Babe can you bring me a beer?" He grunts from the couch. I act like I don't hear his ass and keep right on doing what I'm doing. "Babe, did you hear me?"

"Yes, I heard you Chavon." I answer as dryly as possible to make a point he obviously doesn't get.

"Well…are you gonna get me a beer?" He asks with a hint of attitude.

"That would be a no." I reply indifferently.

"Why not?" He asks like he's mad.

"Because you're not doing anything so you can get up and get yourself a beer. I'm washing dishes and cooking. You've got it."

"See Kyla, I try to get close to you and look how you do." He grunts staggering into the kitchen and getting that damn beer.

"How the hell is asking me to stop what I'm doing to get you a beer while you lay on the couch doing absolutely nothing an attempt to get close to me, Chavon?" I ask checking my pots on the stove with my back to him.

"Because…" he hisses as he sneaks up behind me and plants his mouth softly on my shoulder. "You, giving me the beer was my way of getting you next to me. I was gonna reach out and grab you around your waist to pull you as close as I can get you." He whispers as he slowly wraps both arms around my waist, while gradually stoking my torso seductively cupping both my breasts. His breathing on my neck and the sensation of his touch instantly makes my panties moist, even after all these years. I take in deep breaths just relishing in his touch before speaking. He knows that shit turns me on.

"So, is this what you do to all your women to make them forget how foul you've been to them?" I let fall out of my mouth callously without much forethought. The heat between us instantly goes ice cold, and I can swear I can feel his erection disappear up against my backside at that very moment. And just like that, the moment is lost, and we are back at odds again.

"Damn Kyla! Is it always going to be like this? You gonna fuck up every moment I try to get back to us forever?" Chavon shouts cracking open his beer as he backs away from me. He just leans up against the kitchen island and stares at me like he feels sorry for me.

"I'm sorry. I didn't mean to say that." I back-peddle half-heartedly. In truth, I meant what I said. I just didn't mean to say it out loud that's all. "Look I'm trying Chavon?"

"Trying to do what Kyla, because I am trying to fix us, but you keep fucking us up?"

"No, you keep fucking up! And I keep trying to forgive you for it!" I shout facing him now with my hands on my hip.

"That's where you mess up right there Kyla. You said you're trying to forgive me when it's not an either, or situation baby. Forgiveness is something you do, or you don't do, not something you try to do. So, if you're still trying…what the fuck are we doing?" He utters sadly, almost regrettably with less boom but way more emotion in his expression. He's about as raw as he can be, and I don't know what to say. Then the doorbell rings and saves us both.

Chavon goes to the door and me…well, I pour a much-needed glass of wine and make my way into the foyer to great our guests. When my college bestie, Cierra "Cee-Cee" Folsom struts her stuff into the room my spirit instantly calms. When my husband's homie, Juan saunters in behind her, both Chavon and I are taken aback. Being the Band Director and Auxiliary Coordinator there have been rumors for years about Cee-Cee and Juan's closeness. Many think they have had a secret love affair brewing for years, but it has never been proven. But now, they are looking a little too close for comfort.

"Uhm, what's this? We expected Juan but I didn't know you were going to be joining us Cee-Cee." Chavon stutters taking my girl's sweater as she hands him a bottle of wine.

"Oh, we didn't come together or nothing like that. Kyla told me to swing by for dinner earlier. Juan just pulled up right behind me." Cee-Cee explains pleasantly walking over to hug me after hugging and kissing Chavon.

"Yeah, you know I've got a permanent spot at yawl table on Monday nights. This is our regular. Ain't that right, Kyla?" Juan boasts.

"Right, Juan." Kyla cosigns dryly.

"Anyway, Juan man you are just in time to try this new Cognac I ran across and you know I've got the Cubans on deck, so you down to get it in before we eat?" Chavon teases.

"Oh, hell yeah, Bro. Lead the way, long as there is no more shop talk Von."

"Bro I am way ahead of you. No more shop talk. Now come on." Chavon agrees as he and Juan go off to his little man cave in the basement. That leaves Cee-Cee and I to have a little sister time while I finish up dinner.

"He kills me snatching up the fellas to smoke like we sistas don't indulge." Cee-Cee gripes sipping the glass of Cabernet I just poured her while propped up on a stool at my kitchen island.

"Right, little does my silly husband know…but I like to get in a puff or two every now and then. If his ass wasn't always working, he'd know that by now." I retort sourly.

"Since when Mrs. Goody Two Shoes?" She squeals over giggles.

"Girl, I get my smoke on too just not no damn cigars!" I announce in a hushed whisper as I pull a joint out my apron pocket. "The food's ready so, I'm headed out to the sun porch. You trying to smoke?"

"Hell yell! This reminds me of the good old days Kyla." She answers happily and off we go.

Once settled in on the couch with some jazz blowing in the background it does not take long for Cee-Cee, and I to get lifted. Just two puffs a piece and we are cool, calm and most collected.

"So, what's been happening with you lately Cee? I've been so tied up with the university's homecoming efforts I don't know if I am coming or going. Feels like a million years since we have talked."

"Nothing really Sis. Girl these new budget cuts have me stressing. In all the years I've been working for HSU, 2020 damn near took me out of here. Now that everything is coming back into action, its hard trying to keep up, you know?"

"Yeah, I know but I was talking about your personal life Cee-Cee. What's going on with that?"

"What personal life? Child bye. Ain't nobody got time for that. The HSU Aux is my life and I take that shit very personal." She professes lighting the joint again.

"Yes, yes, I know how dedicated you are to the Aux Program, hell who doesn't? But Cee you are still a young, vibrant, vivacious young woman. Don't you miss the comfort of a man in your life?" I plead with her to open-up and holla at her Sis. It's been way too long since we've done this.

"Kyla, I have come to terms with love not being for me. There was Gerald…"

"Girl that was a million years ago. You were practically a child yourself back then. You cannot base your entire adult life on a mistake that you made way back then!"

"Just because it was a long time ago, or because I was young doesn't make it any less valid an experience in my life! That my dear sister was the purest love I have ever known, and I haven't found anything that even compares to it since."

"Even all those years you danced for the NBA? You've dated many ball players over the years and none of them gave you love? Whenever we linked up you always seemed happy."

"I was happy Kyla, but not because of the men. I was living my best life. I was dancing, being paid quite well for it, traveling the country and loving and leaving dudes all up and through my travels. But love…yeah that was never part of the equation. I never let that happen."

"Why Cee-Cee?" I say sadly, pouring her another glass.

"Because they could never be him, and I always knew that. Stringing them along wouldn't have been fair, Sis. So, I retired from the team when my body told me to and started at Heritage. Everybody doesn't need a man in their life Kyla." She explains solidly enough, but I know better than this line she's feeding me.

"Maybe not everybody, but that doesn't have shit to do with you. You are just afraid, Miss Folsom, point, blank and the period."

"Hell yeah, and with good reason too." She protests.

"Girl love is gonna get your ass when you least expect it. Watch what I say. Your story is nowhere near over." I preach feeling the wine and the weed now.

"Neither is yours old married lady. How are you and Chavon really, Kyla?" She asks more seriously.

"Girl I don't even know. When I see him at work, his ability to handle his stresses, and keep everyone else calm is sexy to me. But when he tries to touch me that way, all I see in my mind is him kissing her. I know he said nothing else happened, but that ain't the way he was kissing her. And Dream hasn't spoken three words to him in weeks. I don't even know what to do anymore. I'm just free-falling." I confess emptying the bottle.

"First of all, she kissed him Kyla and his guilt is fucking with him tougher than you ever could. He doesn't want that skank. You know for Chavon Turner, since I've known him, it's always been only you for him. You said you forgave him."

"I'm fucking trying to Cee-Cee, but it hurts shit! Dream and I saw that shit and I give less than a fuck about her initiating the kiss! He didn't snatch away! He kissed her back and that is the fucking problem. Trust me if I could stop my mind from seeing that shit I would!"

"Well try picturing yourself without the love of your life and see how alone that shit makes you feel. This alone shit is not what you want. Trust me." She finishes and I have no response. She leaves something on my mind with that one and I have no more to say.

****

Chavon

"Juan man I am running out of ideas. Kyla says she forgives me, but she will not let me touch her. Dream is still not speaking to me, and all this is happening even after I fired the bitch!" I confess to my homeboy. Right now, we are not colleagues, just boys.

"You've got to give both Kyla and Dream time Chavon. Kyla sees another woman kissing her husband and Dream saw some tramp bitch slobbering all over her damn Daddy! Nigga that's a lot. You sure you didn't smash?" Juan inquires suspiciously.

"Nawl nigga! Okay, I'm not gone lie Juan. I was attracted to Michelle. Shit she's bad as hell, but I never did anything to make her think I wanted to get with her. I mean yeah, I may have confided in her a few times when Kyla had pissed me off. And yeah, we ate lunch together a few times, but I always remained professional." I maintain seriously passing him the blunt.

"Ain't shit professional about a successful black man complaining about his wife to his single, fine-as-fuck assistant Dog. I don't give a damn what you say!" Juan contends staring hard at me over his glasses.

"Says the man who pushed his wife out the door with his doggish ass shenanigans!" I shoot back at him for analyzing my shit too closely.

"That's exactly why I know what I'm talking about in reference to your shit. Remember, we're not talking about me. We are talking about you."

"I just want my fucking family back man." I admit to my friend sadly.

"Then keep your head in the game and don't let up. Keep fighting for your family man because if I had done that shit, I would not be sitting butt-hurt and fucked up now missing my ex." He confesses sucking down the rest of his Remy XO.

"You still miss her huh?"

"Like a muthafucka, every goddamn day, Dog. I dream about her. I think about her all the damn time. She left some of her clothes in the drawer and they still smell like her. It's been two years Dog, and I still can't shake her."

"Damn Dog. Why don't you just go tell her that shit? You know where she is."

"I promised I wouldn't try anymore. She said if I loved her ever, then I would leave her alone to find her happiness without me. Hell, I figured after all my shit, I owed her that. So, I married the band after the divorce and haven't looked back for shit else but regret." He explains.

"Maybe you need to get back in the saddle. You know they say the best way to get over a woman is to get up under a new one." I joke half-heartedly because I know better.

"Man please, pussy ain't even pleasing to me no more." Juan confesses and my eyebrows raise with the quickness.

"You trying to tell me something nigga?" I warn his ass with my eyes.

"Nawl fool! I mean I don't want no random ass no more. I want my heart back. But Hayley's got it and I don't want it without her! I know that shit now!" He professes as his eyes fill with water. Of course, he catches himself before a tear drops, but seeing him get that close lets me know just how truthful he's being. And if I don't want to be just like his ass, I better stay in this fight for the ones I love or else chance losing out on the best of everything for good.

Chapter 10
No Way to Outrun the Inevitable Destiny

"Now just because you weaseled your petite behind out of being my driver for our VIP's don't think your ass is slick." My Aunt, Kyla barks at me sweetly like only a Boss Lady of her caliber can do. But I don't mind though. She and my mom have their careers riding on the success of tonight's Hall of Fame Banquet and I am always down to be a part of helping them win.

"I don't know what you're talking about TT." I whine back batting my lashes and pretending to be clueless. She's not buying the act though despite how funny I'm being.

"Oh yes you do. I told your prissy behind I wanted you to be my day driver for the van since you know the airport surroundings so good. Yet somehow, Dream ended up doing it. Now how do you explain that?"

"Easily TT, we were still in the middle of setting up the dining room and to be honest, I wanted to finish the tables and gift bags myself as I am more detailed oriented about that kind of stuff than Dream is. So, I asked her to drive this afternoon and I will have her back for driving duties this evening for you. Now looking at the room aren't you glad I made that decision?"

"Well…it does look awesome in here and the VIP area is gorgeous. Those gift bags set the entire table off. What's in them?" She gushes and just like that I have successfully managed to redirect her nosey ass energy.

"All our sponsor products and promotional items like key chains, flashlights, pens, magnets and business cards. Little useful things people never bother to buy but always keep using," I explain like the perfect little intern for her Event Coordinating company that just so happens to hold a hefty contract with the university. Like I explained before my people are mad connected.

"Good job Niecy-Pooh, I am seeing I taught you well." She gushes and I sop up all the accolades as I put the unsuspected final touches on my own money-making plans while finishing the VIP table. I make sure to drop two business cards promoting the escort website in all the male gift bags on the VIP table only. I've already sent anonymous emails to the richest and raunchiest of invitees expected to be here this week so, now may the waiting game begin for connections. As sexy and sophisticated as Jazmeen hooked up the site the last time I checked it, I am sure it won't be long.

"Yes, you did TT. I learn from the best." I cosign grinning from ear to ear.

"So, what did you girls come up with for saving the season for the Auxiliary? I see how that whole thing had you stressing." She asks like the physic I've always thought she was because she can always peep my moods without me saying a word.

"We voted to do a calendar featuring all three groups; The Honeys, Flags & Majorettes."

"Well, it better not be any raunchy mess Destiny. You know your Aunt Cee-Cee is not going for that." She warns me sternly.

"No worries TT, I'm planning the photo-shoots, so you know it's gonna be nothing but sexy sophistication. Come on now."

"Yes, yes I am so sorry Niecy Pooh, I forgot who I was talking to."

"You also forgot to send somebody to pick up your girl from the damn airport!" A tall, caramel, slender but stacked woman looking to be in her late 30's, early 40's yells from across the room with a large suitcase in toe. She looks somewhat familiar, but I can't place who she could be until I hear my aunt's response.

"OMG Ananda Lolita Harris! Get your ass over here!" She yells as they both scream and rush into the cutest embrace. It's cute because they give one another one of those ultra-tight, sway side-to-side hugs that makes people feel all warm and gooey inside just watching it. I love when my mom and aunt get together with their college friends. It's fun watching them let their hair down and cut loose occasionally. The Mansfield-Turner women are always the picture of appropriateness. At least they always work extra hard to be. Their homies, however, always have a way of making them keep it real and I love that part too.

"You are looking like mad money, Sis!" Ananda gushes as she lets go of my aunt just long enough to look her over from head to toe before hugging her again.

"I can say the same about you two-time MVP! You look great too! And for the record I did not forget to send someone to pick you up heifer! You're at least three hours early! What's up with that?"

"Girl, they had room on an earlier flight and since I was there early because of all this Covid mess, I jumped on it switched my luggage and took a Lyft to the yard. That's what happens when a sister can't wait to get home. You know what I'm saying Little Sis?" She explains happily referring her comments to me.

"Yes, Ma'am I totally get what you're saying." I answer her politely.

"Oh, my goodness, I am being so damn rude. Ananda this is my favorite niece, Destiny LeLani Turner and Des, this is my very good friend…" My aunt starts and I finish her statement cutting her off.

"Ananda Lolita Harris #43 for the Detroit Shock and then for the LA Sparks. Two-time Championship MVP, four-time All Star and one time Olympian! And quiet as its kept, I am her only niece," I offer excitedly like a crazed fan. "I am a huge fan as you can see." I continue offering my hand to shake. She smacks my hand down and pulls me in for a tight hug.

"Girl we don't shake hands around Heritage. We hug when its family. Damn you are the spitting image of your father. Cherod couldn't deny you if he tried. You are gorgeous!" she gushes making me blush real hard. After we hug, Ms. Harris gets right down to business.

"Okay enough of the mushy stuff. Put me to work. I'm here early and I know your worker bee behind has got a laundry list of shit that still needs to be done before tonight, right?" Ananda jokes at my aunt's expense.

"No actually we are ahead of schedule so you can just make your way to the hotel and rest up before the banquet. No VIP of mines will be working before this event." My aunt explains right back in party coordinator mode, all work and no tolerance or time for play. "We've just gotta wait for my daughter, Dream to get back with the van."

"I can take her TT." I offer genuinely.

"No, you still have classes so move that ass! Miss Heritage State still needs to make the grade. You're already getting a short week, so you go handle that business." She offers with a smirk totally shooting down my attempts to get out of going to class. *Sometimes I hate it that she knows me so well.*

"Aww man." I say defeated as I gather up my book bag and purse to head to class. As I say my goodbyes, I see Dream coming in with none other than the Host of the smash hit TV show on TV One Vibes & Verses, Anthony Walker! And I must say the brother looks even sexier in person than he does on TV. *Damn if I were just 15 years older.* I think to myself oblivious to my own drooling. Now I really don't want to go to class.

"Hey Mom," Dream announces pleasantly as I watch my aunt's eyes bulge with surprise at the sight of Dream and the VIP she sent her to pick up! So, you know I must stay to watch the show, right?

"Dream, what are you all doing back on the yard? I told you to take our very special guest to his hotel upon his arrival." She fusses with a huge smile. As she walks right up to Mr. Walker giving him a big hug. He smiles hard as he kisses my aunt on the cheek. That infectious smile disappears the moment he looks over my aunt's shoulder to see Ms. Harris standing behind her. *Aww you can't pour and melt my ass out of this room now. I ain't going nowhere.* I ponder as I standby to watch a whole other story unfold.

"Well look who the wind blew in." Ms. Harris comments sardonically smiling after making eye contact with Mr. Walker. I can't tell if she's a fan or something more.

"Well, hello to you too." He replies smugly letting my aunt go.

"Okay I know how this looks but please believe me when I tell you I was not trying to bring you two together, okay?" My TT explains with sincerity as the VIPs fall short of hugging each other. They just kind of nod and keep it short and cordial. They must have mad history.

"No worries Kyla. I am the one who changed up your well-put-together plans to come here on the yard. I figured I'd try to walk down on my son before heading to the hotel." Mr. Walker explains.

"Well now I'ma have to mess up the plan to get you all over to the surprise bar-b-que my husband and Cherod have going on at our house right about now!" My aunt's bestie, and HSU First Lady, Tina Hutchins-Smith announces as she prances happily up on the scene making a b-line straight to Miss Ananda and Mr. Walker. "Nanni! You look amazing!

And Anthony success looks awesome on you!"

"Hey First Lady! Damn I can't believe I am saying that!" Mr. Walker yells as he lifts the First Lady off her feet when they hug.

"I know right? I mean we were all there when she and Eric got married but who would have thought they'd become the President and First Lady of our alma mater? Hey Sis! It's been way too long!" Miss Ananda says as she hugs First Lady too.

"It sure has. Thank you both for coming to participate in this week's festivities. It means the world to both Eric and I."

"Stop it. I would have done this for free. That's how much you both and this university means to me." Mr. Walker tells her kindly. While I watch Miss Ananda roll her eyes as he speaks.

"Yeah, but I am sure you had no problem accepting that hefty check they gave your ass though, huh Super Star? She jokes and everyone giggles barely hearing the dig she follows up with. "Lord knows your ass never offered to return any of my checks back to sender." She mumbles only half audibly under her breath and my TT subtly smacks her hand.

"Well as she should Ananda…as you both should. Alumni or not, this is still about handling our business, right?" First Lady attempts to smother the fire burning between the VIPs but I am here for it. "Now look, I have a class, but I just had to step over here to summons you all to the President's house for lunch. This is not an offer, it's a requirement, so the men are waiting for you all and I will meet you after my classes. Dream please be sure to get Ms. Harris and Mr. Walker over to our house in one piece. Oh, and there is no need to go trying to creep up on Andre`. He has English Lit with me in about 10 minutes and then he'll be meeting you both at my house after class. So, yawl are just gonna have to tolerate each other and be nice enough to leave that boy alone." She announces like the boss she is.

"Oh, is that so?" Ms. Ananda rebuts with her hands on her hips as a smile creeps across her face.

"Yes, that's so and Final. Now that the First Lady has spoken, the Professor has got to bounce. See you guys in a few hours. Oh, and I am really happy you both are here, and I know Andre` will be too."

"Thanks Tina." Both Mr. Walker and Ms. Harris say in unison as they hug her again before she walks off.

Just then my TT's phone buzzes and she steps to the side to take the call, but not before trying to shoe me off to class. I see her make the hand motions for me to get going, but I stall, as long as I can because the VIPs are left to talk.

"You know for the record, those checks you sent were ordered for the care of your son, not required by me." Mr. Walker says with a stiff smile through gritted teeth as soon as First Lady and TT are out of earshot. But I heard him.

"Oh, damn Anthony I was just joking. I didn't mean anything by it." Ms. Ananda back peddles with attitude. "You don't have to take everything so damn seriously."

"Well one of us has to take shit seriously sometimes Ananda! Everyone doesn't always get everything they want like you!" He snaps at her and the look on her face speaks in volumes.

"Fuck you, Anthony." She spits back like a dagger and my TT returns just in time to stop their madness.

"Okay, so let's get you all over to Tina and Eric's house. Dream Honey! Come on babe." She calls out to my cousin as she steps right between them like she knows she's disrupting a war of words as she guides them to the HSU van for transport. Damn, for once, I wish I had Dream's job because I can tell that a hostile party between the VIPs was just getting started.

Chapter 11
Too Much is Said in Not Enough Time Dream

Since my mom had banquet details to attend to, that leaves me to drive Mr. Walker and Ms. Harris to the president's house where my Godparents and Uncle have set up the bomb bar-b-que for them. I don't mind doing it but the tension in this van is thick as shit and these two don't seem to like each other much. Whether I want to or not, I think I'm about to find out what their deal is as we ride because there is nowhere for them nor me to hide.

"Look Anthony I didn't mean to offend you earlier. I was just joking." Ms. Ananda starts politely. But it doesn't take a genius to see that Mr. Walker isn't buying it after he smacks his lips.

"It wasn't funny Ananda." He retorts dryly. "You made it seem like I asked you for those checks. I never asked you for shit! I did whatever it took to take care my son!"

"I never said you did ask for it! As a matter of fact, as I recall I am the one who put the custody agreement in place. I did that to make sure our son would always be taken care of. No matter who he lived with." Ms. Harris retorts back with fire in her eyes.

"Hell, that was the least you could do after dumping me and abandoning your son for the WNBA!"

"First of all, I didn't abandon my son. I let him live with his father so he could have roots and a stable home rather than live out of a fucking suitcase being with me! As much as the league moved me around, he was better off in Atlanta and so were you!" She yelled.

"I never said that Ananda!" He shouted.

"No Anthony, you just told me to go!"

"But I didn't think you would! I thought you loved Dre` and I too much to go, but the joke was on me because the next thing I knew you were gone, and I was Mr. Mom indefinitely." He shouts and she is speechless for a minute that doesn't last long. I hate that I am hearing their dirty laundry, so I just keep my eyes on the road.

"And you did a great job Anthony! Dre`
wouldn't be here at Heritage without you!
And Andre` isn't the one who seems to have
the problem with me, just you!" She screams
in resistance to his rants.

"Oh really? You think I'm the only one who
has a fuckin problem with you? Let's just see
if I am the only one with a fuckin problem,
shall we?" He states heatedly as he pulls out
his cell and starts dialing. He puts the volume
on speaker so everyone in the van, including
little ole me, can hear while he video chats
with their son.

"Yeah?" A young dude's voice grunts
annoyed like he's being interrupted from
something.

"Ah, yeah? Is that any way to answer your
father's call, Andre`?" Mr. Walker poses with
authority staring Ms. Harris down.

"Ahh, sorry Pops. I'm uhm, ahh, I'm ahh just
waking up." He stutters out of breath or
something. He sounds weird.

"Waking up? Boy its damn near two o'clock in the afternoon what do you mean you're just waking up?"

"Ahh, I mean uhm, I had a break between classes man, damn ahh." He huffs like he's in pain or something.

"Are you alright son?" He asks.

"Ahh yeah Pops. What do you need? I'ma bout to get ready for class, ahh."

"Well after class you need to meet me at your Uncle Eric's house."

"Yea, ok, ahh…"

"Andre` is everything okay son? Why do you keep grunting like that? Andre!"

"Huh? Oh yea, ahh I'm cool."

"Well, your mother's gonna be there. You hear me."

"Ahh yeah." He replies obviously preoccupied. That's when I guess Ms. Harris has had enough as she snatches Mr. Walker's arm to put his camera on her.

"Andre` did you hear what your father said?" She asks sternly and when the sight of his mother comes into view it must have startled the living shit out of Andre` because the next thing I know both Mr. Walker and Ms. Harris get the shock of their lives when a female voice yells in unison with their Son.

"Momma?" Both Andre and some girl with her blonde ponytail all in his crouch yells as she unexpectedly pops into the video chat frame, totally shocking this boy's parents smeared lip stick and spit running from her mouth and all.

"What the fuck? I know you don't have some thot in their sucking your little scrawny ass dick?" Ms. Ananda shouts at the tops of her lungs pushing the phone away and covering her eyes.

"Momma, Dad it's not what it looks like! Andre` scrambles to compose himself while juggling and fumbling with his pants, the thot and the phone. It is taking every bit of restraint I have not to bust out laughing. But I know that's not the move when I see the embarrassment on both his parent's faces.

"Oh really, how is it not what it looks like son? What were you doing huh, brushing her throat and tonsils with your man tool, Fool?" Mr. Walker shouts. "Get your shit together and get to that fucking English Lit class you're missing before I kill your stupid ass!" He shouts before ending the call and staring over at Ms. Harris in disbelief.

"Seems he is not the only one with a problem is he old Perfect Powerful Parent, Sir?" Ms. Harris announces boldly as we finally pull up to the house.

As soon as the van stops, Mr. Walker jumps out the car, slams the door and stomps up the walkway towards the house without even grabbing his luggage. Ms. Harris takes her sweet time getting out the car, slightly giggling.

"Come on, Dream let's get this reluctant reunion started, shall we?" She laughs as she meets me in front of the van with a wide smile locking her arm through mine. "Don't trip on what you just witnessed. This weekend is sure to bring a lot of shit to light for sure. So, buckle up Sweetie. We're all in for one bumpy-ass ride this here weekend. Please believe it.

Chapter 12
Welcome to the Hall of Fame
Spiritually Speaking (Angel)

It's the night of the Hall of Fame banquet and everything is set up perfectly, socially distanced yet elegant just like the Turner women arranged. They called in all their on-campus troops to pull hosting duties too. Starting with Miss HSU herself, Destiny sitting at the registration table with Dream passing out name tags while secretly staking out the ballers in the room. The site is making movement already and two dates have already been booked for tonight. As it turns out, Jazmeen was right. Each, and every fickle-ass female that had their nose up at the Aux meeting, reached out privately to roll with the plan. She even got a few fellas in on the fun because it's like Cindy Lauper says, *Girls Just Want to Have Fun* too. So, with things looking up, she has a reason to be sipping cabernet in quiet celebratory reflection.

Scanning the room, she notices a tall, dark and lovely masculine masterpiece sitting at the bar. From afar she pegs him to be in his early forties but, still looking quite youthful, yet distinguished at the same time in a dark grey suit. Destiny takes a long look and is more than just pleased with what she sees. Her stares catch his attention and when his eyes meet hers, he too is pleased with what he sees and wastes no time making it known. He simply nods his head to her, winks and smiles all in one smooth, subtle gesture that is missed by most in the room. However, the intended target got the message loud and clear, and the initial connection is solidified.

Tables down front, closest to the stage are reserved for the President's Family, Administration and Special Guests like our VIPs. That said, the collection of people having to make nice regardless of how they really feel about each other, is staggering. The Turners, both sets and their parents, President Smith's Family, along with their good friends Cierra Folsom and VIP, Ananda Harris are all present and accounted for. Kyla, Dream's mom has all their children working the event so the adults can mingle freely. Since her event planning Company, Kreative Events by Kyla LLC holds the special events contract with Heritage, and her sister, Kayla's, Destiny's mom's PR Firm handles HSU marketing for events, she's got it like that. The mood is pleasant as the presentations continue with the evening's host, Anthony Walker engaging the crowd.

"Ladies and Gentlemen, allow me to introduce the man with the master plan, the newly named President of Heritage State University, and a damn good friend of mines, Dr. Eric Smith!"

Eric proudly struts to the podium to a monster applause to do a job he has been looking forward to secretly for quite some time and now is the time to reveal another facet to his transition plans for Heritage. His stomach may be in knots, but his outlook is promising and hopeful as he takes to the mic.

"It's usually the job of the Director of Athletics to announce the inductees into the Hall of Fame and while I know Coach Fuller is full of admiration and pride for our next honoree, I am honored he stepped aside to allow me to make this very special presentation. Ananda L. Harris is more than just one of our esteemed successful alumnae. She is an example of perseverance, dedication and staying power. She struggled in the early days of her college career and fought her way back to school to soar to prominence in all she did here at Heritage. Leading both our Women's Basketball and Volleyball teams to multiple championships, while maintaining an impressive grade point average for three consecutive years, Ananda's drive has always been unmatched. Her philanthropic efforts after graduating to advance the opportunities for women in sports and education here at Heritage have resulted in a new track and workout facility, along with numerous endowments and scholarship efforts.

On a personal level, as a student I watched her deal with trials and rise above to soar far beyond everyone's expectations. We truly applaud all her professional triumphs on and off the court. It's because of her work that I am humbled and honored to Induct #43 Ms. Ananda Lolita Harris into the Heritage State University Sports Hall of Fame Class of 2021 with an invitation to join the HSU family in the role of Women's Basketball Head Coach! Ms. Harris please come accept your award and hopefully a job offer as we would love to turn this night into a celebration of your matriculation back home!" Eric boasts with a smile a mile-wide spread across his face. Upon finishing the audience explodes in thunderous applause as the spotlight shines on the table where Ananda is sitting down front.

When Eric's offer finally registers, Ananda is moved to tears and stillness unable to move to get her award. She is shocked and moved in ways she is not fully equipped to handle. Seeing her struggling, Eric steps off the stage and walks over to her table with a hand extended to help her to the podium. When he gets in front of her and she takes his hand, the applause grows even louder as she hugs Eric tightly before finally making her way to the stage. With a trembling voice Ananda takes to the mic.

"Never in a million years did I expect anything like this. I am so humbled by this induction and truthfully, shocked by this job offer. I know it was no accident that I get this news in front of you all as I am sure the powers that be know putting me on the spot like this is the best way to get their bottom line met." She explains as the crowd erupts with laughter. "I am thankful that Heritage took a chance on me and groomed me for a life in professional sports. I learned lessons here that I took with me all over the world and still apply to this day. It has always been my mission to give back to the institution that gave me so much and now it looks like you all have provided me with a means to do just that. I humbly accept your invitation to Coach the Women's Basketball team and I am sure that Dr. Smith will make my compensation worth my wild. This is wild. I Love You, I Trust you, and I Respect you all immensely from the bottom of my heart. For God, For Faith, For Heritage!" She emotionally pledges as she takes her plaque and new job offer back to her seat at the table with hugs and accolades coming from every direction.

As soon as Ananda makes her way back to her seat Cierra, Kyla and Tina all rush her with hugs and for a split second the scene reminds them of their own college days at Heritage. Each happy to see the other win. The only faces that aren't too enthused by the news of Ananda's now indefinite, extended stay in the area are the evening's host, Anthony and their son, Andre` Walker, the ladies-man wanna-be, sophomore who conveniently abandoned his usher duties to puff a blunt in the parking lot during his mom's speech with Eric and Tina's kids. He vents to his friends while they hotbox his 2014 navy-blue Ford Explorer Sport fully loaded. It appears Mom and Dad did agree on one thing, their son's privilege.

"Man, it's bad enough I have to play nice with my absentee mother all this week, but now's she's gonna be coaching here?" Dre` complains as he puffs and passes to Erin Smith, the socially conscious, slightly insecure but exotically gorgeous, brainiac Junior with her mother's quick wit and her father's ambition, EJ's older twin.

"I had a chance to chill and vibe with your mom earlier at the bar-b-que and for real Dre`, she's not as bad as you make her out to be. She's pretty chill to me." She explains sweetly passing the puff to EJ.

"Yeah, and maybe if you work on your Mommy issues, you all can work on being a family," EJ counters with optimism and promptly gets shut down.

"Man, that ship sailed away a long ass time ago. I am doing me to death and fuck the rest! I ain't got no damn mommy issues either, Nigga!" Andre` demands fiercely letting the siblings know to leave the subject right there.

Just then the trio is startled by sudden, rapid tapping on the driver's side window. It's so smoky in the ride that they can't see who it is through any of the windows, so Andre` is forced to roll his window down. When he does and the plum of endo smoke clears, they are all shocked to see Ms. Cierra Folsom, Auxiliary Coordinator and unofficial Auntie to all three of them staring back at them in disbelief.

"Seriously children? This is what your asses is doing while your folks are in there hosting and accepting awards Andre`, and passing out job opportunities Erin and EJ? Are you all out of your fucking minds?" Cierra yells to them like the cool-ass Auntie she is, that is working hard not to ask to hit that fat ass blunt herself.

"Aww Auntie Cee-Cee we caught the best part of the presentation." Erin chokes out blowing smoke right into her aunt's direction after trying to hold it in too long.

"Erin honey I am going to act like you did not just say that dumb shit to me. Now put that shit out, freshen the fuck up as best you can, pop an Altoid, and get your Friday franchise high asses back up in there now! And I better see yawl helping until the very end or else I am singing like a canary to all parents, even the visiting ones." She commands to the group stressing her last words to Andre`.

"But Aunt Cee, it's not fair that the person who has the least to do with my upbringing gets to make decisions that impact my life and I'm just supposed to roll with it? That's foul man." Andre` finally confesses.

"I feel where you're coming from Nephew but until you make some noise no one will ever hear you. You know what I'm saying?" Cee-Cee carefully explains in the most nurturing tone she can muster with the new contact buzz she's experiencing.

"I hear you, Aunt Cee…but damn," he hisses as he blows the last puff before putting the blunt in his aunt's hand.

"Well, if you're going to go easy on him, then you've gotta give us some slack too Auntie. EJ and I have been sitting front row center for our parents fighting like they're on Real World Grown and Sexy edition for weeks! And when they aren't attacking each other, they're throwing us in the middle of their shit! That's why we need to smoke to mellow out the madness!" Erin explains passionately hoping to convince her aunt not to snitch on them.

"Please! Have you ever stopped to think about the constant pressures your parents deal with on the daily? Do you think it's easy prioritizing the needs of an entire university while managing a household, kids and a spouse? All of this is new to them. Give them a little room to get used to being in such high demand. Hell, they could probably use a smoke break or two their damn selves! Did either one of you over-accommodated geniuses ever even think of that?" Cee-Cee suggests another way of looking at their situation and the twins plus one begin to finally hear her.

"Nawl, Aunt Cee-Cee, neither one of us has ever looked at it like that." EJ admits remorsefully.

"Right, I know you all didn't. Now go get your asses back in there, and be of some assistance rather than the resistance," She orders of the three stooges with a grin and they all file back through the parking lot into the hall.

Once the gang is safely back inside, after scanning the parking lot noticing its empty, Cierra checks to be sure no one is watching before taking a puff from the blunt she confiscated from the youngins. After her exhale, she goes to hit it again and notices the flame is out. Before she can check her purse for a lighter, a flame quietly dances in her peripheral vision. She looks over her shoulder only to see the guy from the bar offering her a much-needed light. To her, he looks like something out of a movie in his dark grey suit up close. She's startled and intrigued at the same time once again when he smiles at her.

"Need a hot flame?" he smoothly whispers into her ear.

"What are you doing following me?" She asks coyly holding his hand steady as she lights the blunt. After a long drag and a gracious thank-you, he answers her.

"Would it get me brownie points if I said I was?" He jokes.

"No, it would probably get you arrested. I don't do stalkers."

"Well then it's a good thing I've got a friend in there being inducted tonight. What's your excuse to be out here looking delicious while puffing grass in the dark?" He inquires curiously.

"The same. But as for the smoking, we'll just call that a bonus." She jokes with an innocent smile.

"Well, you know sharing is caring." He says seductively making Cierra blush. That's when he knows he's got her attention.

"Oh, I would have thought you were too cool for this?" She says before passing it to him casually exhaling in his direction.

"How do you think I keep it so cool?" He jokes as he puffs and then passes it back to her. As he watches her inhale and exhale, he cannot stop his mind from wondering what her body looks like naked. The liquor he's been tossing back all night is beginning to take control and she is working his hormones up into a quiet frenzy just watching her. After his last hit, he just throws caution to the wind and decides to shoot his shot.

"Look Eve, I don't like to beat around the bush, and I don't believe in coincidences. Us meeting and running into each other tonight has got to be fate. So why don't you let me take you out like real grown folks do?" he says in a mildly sensuous tone with a seriously sexy stare that seems to see right through her. As curious as this man makes her, Cierra is still apprehensive about getting better acquainted.

"I wish I could, but I can't. I've gotta get back inside. I'm on breakdown duty when all this is over since my friends are the organizers." She issues sweetly before she turns and begins to walk away. He gently grabs her wrist to stop her.

"So, you're turning me down cold again, huh?" He asks as he softly strokes her arm before grabbing her hand as he steps closer to her. "I was hoping I could get to know you better Lady."

"Well don't take it personal. It's just bad timing. If it's meant then hope springs eternal, right, Adam?" She suggests coyly flirting.

"That it does Ms. Eve. That it does." He agrees pleasantly as he suavely leans down and sensuously kisses her hand. As he watches her switch her way back inside the hall, he hopes his gesture left something on her mind. He is even more attracted to her now considering the chase is on and if he has anything to do with it this Adam will surely get his Eve in his bed if it's the last thing he does indeed.

****

The night continues with the final inductee presentation of Sheldon Ross, HSU football legend, turned Law Enforcement Officer and Chief of the local police department. For this one, the Director of Athletics, Coach Fuller steps to the mic.

"I want you all to know it really pained me to step aside and allow President Smith to make the last speech considering I have always thought of Ananda Harris as the bonus daughter I never had. However, this next presentation brings my heart just as much joy as our next honoree has always been like a son to me." He explains emotionally. "I have known this man for many years. I have coached him, counseled him and combatted his inner quitter many times. Now I am honored to induct a four-time HSU Football Champion, two-time Track Champion and generous all-around supporter of Heritage Sports, Sheldon R. Ross into the HSU Sports Hall of Fame!"

Chief Ross, a distinguished robust, tall, fair-skinned man, takes long concentrated strides to the stage shaking hands and exchanging pleasantries with people at every table he passes on the way. Anyone can tell he is well known and respected especially at HSU.

"Good evening," He greets in a rich husky tone that captivates the room. "When I was informed of this honor, I was overjoyed. I always dreamed of this day and to be here now as it comes to fruition is proof that dreams do indeed come true. That said, I also feel that it is equally important to pass that feeling forward to someone coming after you. That is why I am happy to announce a $5.1 million- dollar endowment to Heritage State University's General Fund and Athletics Departments in collaboration with The Gilliam Athletic Corporation and United Land Trust Bank! Our intended solution to eliminate financial deficits and expand recruiting efforts to increase diversity!" He announces proudly with his chest stuck way out there as two young ladies appear on stage carrying a large cardboard cut-out of the check he's speaking of. It is at that time that he calls up President Smith and the rest of the evening's VIPs for photo opts.

Although President Smith is all smiles on stage, his better half sits in her seat fuming at their table as she watches her idea of a collegiate circus unfold, and it doesn't take long after dinner starts for her to make her discontent known…publicly no less once Eric makes it back to the table.

"Eric, I know this donation takes a huge weight off your shoulders about getting that debt under control. Congratulations!" Board member, Michael Mansfield boasts loudly.

"Thank you, Mr. Mansfield and yes it does bring my stress level down significantly. We can do so much with the remaining funds once the debt is settled. There is so much that we can *do* for the university." Eric replies excitedly, feeling he has a right to be happy.

"Yes well, it will be very interesting to see how what *you do* for the university effects what you *do to* the university." Tina mumbles under her breath sarcastically just loud enough to be heard by most at the table. Cierra hits her friend's knee under the table as neither reacts.

"Ooh, now that is an interesting point First Lady, please elaborate." Jacqueline Mansfield coaches politely as she sits divided on the issue of what is best for the university. While she is and has been a financial and active HSU

Board of Trustee Member, she is compelled to side with her colleagues, and that includes her husband, Michael. However, unlike Michael, Jacqueline supports boosted alumni/community involvement efforts strongly that support bringing more students of color to HSU. Therefore, she welcomes the chance for a younger, fellow alumnus to state their case in opposition to solely depending upon corporate, multi-cultural-based funding hoping her bull-headed hubby will listen.

"Yes, Honey please but before you start don't forget to mention how the Board's suggestion to pitch to Gilliam Athletics led to this major donation that will finally put HSU in the black and ultimately move us up to higher division conferences for the sports programming. No more Division 3, I'm talking Division 2 and up! Overall, it's a no-brainer, win/win." Eric mentions first as he is sure Tina will not. He glares in her direction and if looks could kill, Eric's head would explode right there at the damn table.

"All true, however I just worry that because affiliation with corporations usually result in strict stipulations for the school that undermine our historically black traditions." Tina explains pleasantly through a smile and gritted teeth.

"Like what?" Mr. Mansfield interjects rudely.

"Like our award-wining Last Chance Student Initiative that has brought HSU national notoriety. Higher division conferences have stricter G.P.A. requirements for not only the sports programs but for overall school admission standards which may hinder or worse, force HSU to eliminate the LCS Initiative altogether. Now where in the world would we be without our alumni that initially benefited from that program like tonight's Host, Mr. Walker here?" Tina further explains and as heads begin shaking all around the table, the agitation that overpowered Tina's expression just minutes ago, is now displayed on Eric's face instead.

In an effort to break up the debate at the table between her parents, Erin coughs and asks to be excused. "Mother do you mind giving me a hand?" She stresses with a fake smile as she gets up.

"Sure Sweetheart," Tina answers sweetly as she rises from her seat. "Please excuse us for a moment." Once mother and daughter depart the table EJ switches the vibe.

"So, Mr. Walker, I had no idea you were a Last Chance Initiative student. Me too. All I know is your show on TV One, Vibes & Verses is dope af!" He announces excitedly. Everyone at the table laughs and he has successfully refined the vibe at the table.

"Yeah, well there would definitely be no show without that Last Chance Student Initiative because coming out of high school, my English and my grades were in the toilet. No other school would touch my foreign ass." He jokes and everyone breaks up laughing again.

"Yeah, and then 20 years later that same program performs the same miracle for your seed!" Andre` announces ironically proud. "I had to put in a lot of hard work my junior and senior years to get here. Had to find motivation from all directions to stay at it but I made it!"

"Yes, you did Son, and I am so proud to say I had something to do with that!" Anthony cosigns with a huge smile as everyone at the table looks on.

"Well..." clearing her throat and sipping her water first Ananda interrupts, "I would like to think that both of us had a little something to do with that!"

"Yeah, well some of us more than others obviously," Anthony counters sarcastically and Ananda feels the proverbial sting from across the table. Everyone can see it's on now. "Some of us stick and stay while others run from the fun and just throw money at their problems!" He mumbles under his breath loud enough to be heard still.

"Well, when only one is making the money, everyone has got to play their position! It was hard as hell but fair, I guess! After all, look what we got in the trade off...a gifted young scholar growing into one helluva success story." She ends sweetly enough, trying to kill the sour in her tone she started this exchange with after peeping the uncomfortable vibe at the table.

"I did the best I could while you just up and ran away! The least you could do is send money to compensate me for my services!" Anthony whispers angrily through gritted teeth forgetting all about his unbothered persona of earlier. His baby's momma has clearly touched a nerve.

"Who ran? I went to play ball! That's what I went to Heritage for Genius, or did we forget? I didn't abandon anyone! You told me to go! You knew how much that dream has always meant to me!" Ananda shouts as her eyes fill with water.

"Yeah, but silly ass me, I thought me, and your son meant more to you than fucking basketball! Yeah, I told you to go, but I never thought you would! What kind of mother can just abandon her son like that?" He hisses.

"For the last fucking time Anthony, I did not abandon my son! I left him with his father! And how long are we supposed to paint roses on your damn chest for simply doing what a parent is supposed to fucking do, huh? Be mad at me for the rest of all time! I don't give a good goddamn! But when it comes to my, I mean excuse me, our son…get your fucking story straight!" She counters seriously without hesitation just above a whisper shutting him completely down from saying another word.

"Now brothers and sisters I sincerely apologize for allowing this conversation to happen like this, here! I hope you all can find it in your hearts to forgive us, but I am going to excuse myself now before I make things much worse. I am so sorry baby." She issues to the entire table and her son specifically before getting up and stomping away.

As everyone is still sitting speechless at the table without a clue as to the appropriate way to move dinner along, Cierra sits living in confusion like the Phyllis Hyman song. She hated to watch all her friends have it out right there at the damn dinner table. Eric and Tina are her favorite couple and Ananda and Anthony still have too much energy between them for anyone else to miss. *It's crazy how people who are supposed to have their shit together, can be so close to letting everything fall apart.* She thinks to herself as she sits at the table stewing over what to do. When she looks up across from her, she sees six eyes fixated on hers, those of EJ, Erin and Andre`. The collective look they are giving her is one she has seen way to often in her travels over the years. It's the look that says loudly without words, "See Auntie Cierra, we told you so!"

Tonight's banquet solidified Eric's new mission for his administration and shows he is a man who knows how to make things happen. With any luck, he will figure out how to bring his star player, his wife, Tina around to his side of the battle before it further divides them. Anthony and Ananda still have issues after 20 + years. What the hell else is new? Hopefully, they will finally put their stuff aside to see what's really up with their son. Then there's the case of what's going to happen with Cierra and the mystery man she keeps running into? Will her curiosity make her explore opening her closed doors to love or at least a little lust? Last, but not least Honey, is Miss Destiny in over her head or working things out like a Pro on the Prowl? What do you think?

It seems as if everyone has a secret agenda of sorts for the weekend, and this Hall of Fame

Banquet is only the beginning of the shenanigans. Well, your Resident Angel thinks there is more to this than meets the eye. However, my mission is still clear. As always, I am here to protect HSU, However, the mission of protection seems to be two-fold. First, we must figure out how an epic history-making Homecoming, turns into the scene of horrified madness in just a few short days? Then, find out who has motives against our beloved Miss HSU, Destiny and how much of the bullshit is really her fault? Keep reading to discover who is trying to commit a Murder on the Yard!

Chapter 13
Favors Have Consequences
Destiny

As this long ass night finally comes to an end, I find myself wanting to get into something naughty. However, looking around the room, I don't see anyone even remotely worth my trouble. That is until I scope out Handsome Elder again, posed at the bar still killing it in that charcoal grey suit. Just as I begin to scheme up a reason to Naomi Campbell walk my ass in that direction, Kayla Mansfield aka Mommy Dearest disturbs my groove.

"Destiny Honey, I've got one more task I need completed before we call it a night." She states more like a formality than a request. Which means she's gonna make me do it.

"Umm Mother, I have been your step and fetch it all day long! Can I please pass this task off to Dream? I am tired." I whine like a first grader, and I am not ashamed…much.

"And? Until you acquire that degree, get a well-paying job that will finally pop my milf-like titty from your mouth once and for all, you will step and fetch for as long as I fucking say so. You got that Darling?" She hisses just above a whisper in my ear.

"Yes Ma'am." I relent with my head down.

"Yeah, that's what I thought." She replies with the duck lips before continuing. "Now one of my gentlemen guests has totally overindulged with the cocktails tonight. Therefore, I need you to drive him to the Marriot in town. I'll make sure he has his room key and wallet, so you won't need to see him into the hotel. Just get him there safely."

"Mother that's too far out in the opposite direction for me to be driving this late!" I protest.

"Destiny! This is important! Now I realize it may be a slight inconvenience, but I would not ask if it wasn't serious! So, save the drama! I am your Mama so be like Nike and just do it!" She demands, and I know its final, so I just snatch my purse of the nearby table and stomp my way out the room. Heading towards the parking lot without another word I am pissed and embarrassed as I hear her yell to me before I get out the swinging glass doors.

"Pull your car up to the front and I will send him right out!" she instructs me. I just shake my head the entire time doing as I am told. Parking right in front of the hall, I wait for my mother's drunken old friend to stagger to my car.

After twenty whole minutes of waiting, I am hot! *Where is this fool on the shitter or something? They better bring their ass on or somebody's gonna get left!* I think to myself getting madder by the minute. The next thing I know I am on my phone punching in my mother's number to see what's taking so long when my eyes deceive me as my passenger side door suddenly opens up. Imagine my surprise to see Handsome Elder of all people slide up in my ride.

"Now this is better than any Uber or Lyft." He sexily slurs with a sinister grin as he settles in my seat. We sit in silence for a moment just staring at each other. I don't know about him, but I am still hot just in other places suddenly.

"You are the friend of my mother that needs a ride?" I ask somewhat dumbfounded.

"That would be accurate. Can you help an old man out?" He asks with that same grin that seems to imply so much more.

"Sure, why not. It's the Marriot, right?"

"Yes, please and thank you in advance." He answers as I pull off.

For the first ten minutes of the drive, we sit in silence as I try to think of something sexy to say without appearing whorish. Before I can come up with anything, he breaks the monotony.

"So, tell me Beautiful, how did you go about convincing your mother to let you drive me back to my hotel?" He asks smugly peering at me.

"What? Umm no Sir, I did no such thing. I was trying to go home when she practically begged me to take her drunken buddy to his hotel." I snap back sarcastically.

"Oh, come on now. You don't have to lie. I know you've been watching me all night. I saw you Sweetheart." He issues obnoxiously and I am flabbergasted. *Seriously? Does this old fart fucking hear himself? He must not know about Destiny!*

"If that were true Sir it means you've been watching me all night! And who could blame you? I am sexy as shit." I counter with much class unfazed.

"That much we can agree on." He snaps back and again we sit in silence as I finally pull up to the hotel main entrance. He looks at me strangely before speaking. "Looks like we're here."

"Yes, and not a minute too soon either. If you will excuse me, its late and I do have other things to attend to." I offer nonchalantly, giving him no eye contact.

"Oh, it's like that, huh? Yep, I knew it. I knew I had you pegged right." He says chuckling as he opens the door to get out.

"What, and how's that?"

"As a big, old, pretty tease! Staring down grown ass men all night never really planning to do shit! Just another young ass girl playing games." He hisses to me, staring me down like he sees right through me. I cannot stop the sensation that look gives me.

"Well, I may be young, but I am old enough to play whatever game your old ass has in mind." I challenge this dude with a sexy stare of my own. He knows not who he is fucking with.

"Oh, is that right?" He asks with a smile as he slams his door back shut. He scopes out the parking lot from various directions before continuing. "Okay Betty Bad-Ass, drive this thing over to that dark corner behind the hotel and I will show you what my old ass has in mind!" He challenges me seriously as his grin disappears with the sexy stare still there.

Without another word, I do as I am told and park the car in the darkest back area of the hotel parking lot. He gets out the car as soon as I stop, and I turn the car off and do the same. We meet face-to-face at the back of the car. Neither of us says a word. Again, I am trying to think of something slick to say since it seems he has suddenly lost all that nerve he was just speaking with, but I've got nothing.

That's when he suddenly makes the first move and snatches me up into a tight embrace, before slamming a yard of tongue down my throat. I am surprised and impressed at the same time as I kiss him back with just as much intensity as he gives me, loving every minute of it. We kiss hard nonstop for what seems like an eternity before he abruptly stops and throws me up onto the trunk of my car. Pushing my back against the window of the car, he boldly pushes his body against mines as he positions himself between my legs and I swallow hard anxious to see what's next.

Never breaking the intense stare-down we now have going on, he slowly slides his hands up my thighs, under my dress, grabbing the sides of my panties. He then looks at me as if to get my permission to proceed. At this moment we are both breathing hard and there are parts of me throbbing for attention like I have never quite felt before. We say nothing but as my underwear begins to slide down my legs, I don't stop him. When he lifts my black, satin panties to his nose, sniffs, and then slides them into his pants pocket with a sly grin, I still don't stop him. He then uses his right hand to massage my nature, gliding his hand back under my dress as he hungrily stares me down. He is pressing his thumb against my clit with just enough pressure to make my thighs tingle and the more turned on he can tell I am, the more he does whatever he wants to me with just one freaking hand. I feel my walls moisten even more when he slides a finger inside of me while still staring me down. My moans grow as he works my body with his hands to make me cum inside of them. As soon as my juices begin to pour, he speeds up his hand's pace until I convulse with pleasure I can barely handle. When he's sure I'm finished, he slides inside of me, lifting me up by my ass cheeks and slowly starts grinding me up and down on his dick. I hold on to his neck tightly while I lose my fucking mind because I can't even remember when he took his dick out! But his stroke is massaging my walls to the point that nothing else matters to me but this moment. Handsome Elder rocks my world on the trunk of my car for the best 15 minutes I have ever experienced sexually before finally putting my feet back down to the ground. My legs are still shaking, and I am at a loss for words as I struggle to calm my breathing. When I look over at him, he has managed to compose himself faster, but he's just as flustered as I am whether he knows if I see it or not. Once I get my faculties together, and he calms down, he takes my hand and walks me back around to the driver's side of the car. He then leans down and kisses me passionately. He stops and just stares at me.

"I guess you're not so young after all huh," he asks with a grin?

"Guess you're not as old as I thought huh," I counter.

"Thanks for the ride...both of them, Miss?"

"You're welcome two times." I offer back slickly.

"So, you're really not going to tell me your name, after what we just did?" He asks ironically with a chuckle.

"Not tonight. See ya later…Sir." I offer getting in my car and starting the ignition. He kisses me on the cheek before slowly backing away from my car.

"That's cool Sweetheart. Until we meet again." He says with that same cool ass smile.

"Will we meet again?" I ask playfully.

"Oh, count on it. We will definitely meet again." He replies before turning and jogging towards the hotel. Once he's in, I drive off tripping on how my mother set me up to get the ride of my life! *Wow, I never knew an older man could make my body feel the way it felt with Handsome Elder. I don't know if it was the fact that it all happened outside, in a dark parking lot on the trunk of my car, or if it was all just the euphoria of being with a stranger. But I can't deny I liked it a lot. I don't even know how much of that there I can take yet, but I am certainly going to figure it out. We will meet up again sooner rather than later for me to figure all this shit out indeed.*

Chapter 14
Situations and Revelations
EJ

Although it is too damn early to have my eyes open, 4 am is the best time to do what I do because the campus is still sleeping, and I can make moves without being seen and that's just how I like it. I do my regular and light the fat ass blunt I rolled for myself last night and commence to puffing as I wait on a bench by the baseball field for my boy, Dorian. We always meet here in the early morning when we have business to handle. He may be only a freshman, but he's smart, cooler than he looks at first glance and he's discreet and that's why I fuck with him. He never keeps me waiting and he is a great fucking customer, one of my best on this campus. So, I always make accommodations for my number ones and Dorian fits that bill. After about ten more minutes, his dorky, light skinned, lanky ass appears out of nowhere.

"What up doe?" He greets me with a pound as he sits, and I pass the blunt to him. He takes a few puffs right away.

"Sup? I thought you forgot about me out here for a minute." I answer him as he passes the blunt back to me.

"Nawl, man. I ain't forget. I need that and then some if you can get your hands on more. I'm talking a lot more." He inquires.

"That may be possible homie, but first thing's first." I say to the little homie as I get up and motion for him to follow me.

We head across campus moving swift in between buildings avoiding all potential opportunities to be noticed if someone is watching which I highly doubt. We take a rarely used path between the two long abandoned dorms on the yard, Ellington and Houghton Halls. Just at the back corner of Ellington is a set of stairs leading to an underground portion of the building I am sure almost no one even knows about. Its real dark so my dude is following real-close, too damn close.

"Damn back up nigga! Your hot ass breath is steaming up the back of my damn neck!" I stress in a whisper laughing but meaning every word.

"Awl, my bad EJ man but for real where the hell are you taking me man?" Dorian, the freshman from Detroit asks in a hushed whisper.

"Awl, I know your murder city ass ain't scared of a few dark alleys now?" I mock. "I am taking you to my office Dorian. You know how when you need to see your professor, you've got to go to their office, right? Well, that's where we're going, to my office to handle private business." I explain as I shuffle down the ten cement steps to a big ass black door. I take out my scissors and pick the lock on the door to let us in. Once behind the door, I lock it from the inside and hit the lights. Dorian's eyes buck open as wide as saucers as he scans the room.

"Man, this is a dope little hide-a-way." Dorian declares ultra-impressed at my set up. And why wouldn't he be impressed? *After all, I do have a quaint little bachelor's room of my very own all to myself. It's got two mattresses with my own 500-threat count, black sheets on it with 2 fluffy pillows, a little bathroom with a sink and toilet, and a desk and chair in the corner. I've got a 200-watt portable power station in here that I use very strategically, a gang of battery- operated lanterns that get bright as fuck, and a small closet on the other corner that I use for my product supply and manufacturing. I guess one could call me enterprising at the very least when you break it all down.*

"Yeah, this is where I handle most of my business, not in the dorms. There it's too many eyes. You know what I'm saying?" I boast handing him his usual ounce of my finest, homegrown weed. He in return drops me that $150 and I slide the ends in my pocket.

"Oh, I am sure you be having chicks down here losing their damn mind over on this side of the yard nobody can hear them screams of passion." Dorian jokes as he puts his package away in his bookbag.

"Dude I could have a slew of chicks down here doing all types of raunchy shit, but that's not where this head is at, Man. If it don't make dollars, it don't make no sense to me, real talk. Nothing more and nothing less. I work best in boss mode." I profess looking at

186

him like he's crazy. I can tell my response surprised him.

"Hold up, no disrespect man, but I heard you come from money. I mean your dad is the president of the damn school!" he says ironically.

"Yeah, but I am not that spoiled ass kid depending on my parent's dime to do my thing. That's played and I'm smart. So, I prefer to make my own ends, so I can make my own way." I explain sitting on the bed and lighting that blunt we were smoking back up.

"Well look here EJ. If you are as much about your money as you say, I may have insight into getting your money up even more." He teases as he hits the blunt after I pass it to him.

"Oh yeah? How?" I inquire curiously.

"Look, I feel you on making your own ends. I don't like to depend on muthafuckas for shit either. That's why I do my thing gambling on the black web. I can do it at my leisure, plus if you know what you're doing, it pays quite well." He explains as he puffs then passes back to me.

"Okay but how does any of that help my situation?"

"All these folks I play with be looking to get lifted and I know you sell that good-good. I can put you in touch with them for a small finder's fee of course, and you can get at this real money." He explains excitedly, but I am still skeptical.

"What do you mean, real money Dorian?" I ask strongly considering his proposition.

"Nigga I mean these folks look to buy bigger than I do, and you already told me I am one of your best customers because I come spending nothing less than $150 a pop. Well, this is how I keep that up and I know at least five of my gambling buddies that I am sure will buy from you bigger than I do! We can make a quiet, smooth killing if you're down." Dorian offers once more, looking at me like a man about his business. Working with him might just take my little enterprise to the next level but I don't know yet. As I am lost in thought and Dorian is just stuck high as fuck in the chair at the desk, we are both startled by rapid knocking on the door. Staring at Dorian, I am instantly pissed off because no one is even supposed to know about this spot much less be bold enough to knock on the fucking door.

Trying to still be quiet, Dorian and I scuffle to put the blunt out, Febreze the room right quick so it's not as obvious what was going on up in here and pop a couple breath mints before answering that damn door. Walking over to it, I snatch the door open hiding the bulk of my body behind it. When I see Destiny's nosey ass in a huge black hoodie over the dress she had on last night at the banquet, I yank her busy ass in the room with the quickness. I better think fast because now, I know I have some explaining to do.

"See, I was just playing when I said I knew you had a secret spot, but your response made me curious and look what we have here. Now, what that hell are you doing down here and what the fuck are you doing with his young ass? Please don't tell me you're on the DL EJ, because that is some ole Empire-esque type shit right there that I am just not here for, okay!" She shouts and I grab her around the neck to cover her mouth and stifle her loud ass interrogation. Destiny peers over at Dorian with much disdain. That's when his fun begins.

"Hey Miss Heritage!" Dorian waves to antagonize Destiny with his Michael B. Jordan in the Black Panther movie impression. When I laugh Destiny is not amused.

"What the hell are you doing down here?" She asks me again without even acknowledging Dorian.

"No, I am the one asking the questions up in here. How the fuck did you know we were down here? And where are you creeping from this early in the morning?" I pose intensely trying to take the pressure off Dorian and me.

"Where am I creeping from? For your information I was just getting in from a long, late night when I saw you all sneaking across campus looking suspicious as hell. So, I followed you! Now what the fuck are you doing with a spare room in the abandoned dorm EJ? I know for sure now your smart ass is up to something. What is it?" She quizzes me intensely. Usually, I don't mind Destiny's interest in my movements because we do go back, and I've still got feelings for her. But I don't know about letting her in on this business.

"Ain't nobody on the Down Low up in here girl and you know it. You ain't forget." I stress giving her the duck lips before continuing. "And this is not a spare room so much as it is my office that nobody else knows about and I know as my girl you're gonna keep it that way, right?"

"Maybe I will, maybe I won't. Who's to say?" She teases as she struts around the room scoping out every visible detail of my set up. "Well tell me this, what's your connection to this lame?" She asks arrogantly pointing to Dorian.

"Oh, I'm a lame now, huh? Funny your fine ass wasn't saying that shit a few months ago when this so-called lame had your damn legs shaking!" Dorian spits back at her with much attitude that clearly pisses Destiny off.

"Don't get checked speaking out of turn youngin." Destiny warns my boy.

"Don't have me crack your face when we both know cracking your back would be way more fun." He replies carelessly without hesitation or remorse blowing out a grand puff of blunt smoke like the exclamation point to his sentence. The comment shocks Destiny and she snaps her head around like a killer poodle on the prowl. Dorian is not holding them up and Destiny is not having any of it. I just stand back and watch the show.

"Let me holler at you for a minute EJ." Destiny says in a hushed whisper as she snatches me up by the arm and guides me out the room. Once she closes the door behind her another investigation begins. "Whatever little secret operation you've got going on over here, you better think twice about letting Boy Wonder in there in on it. You are too old to be pulling freshmen into your hustle don't you think?" She protests.

"Please, that Boy Wonder in there is one of my best customers. Brother spends no less than $150 a pop every time he cops from me. I can set my watch to him, and he always has the ends on lock. Never an issue, plus he's about to hook me with more clients like him so, I am fucking with old boy because it's good for my business Des, emphasis on the word *my*. And how is it you think you know so much about him anyway?"

"Trust me I may not know a lot about him, but I know what I know and he ain't about shit in my book." She insists adamantly.

"Why Destiny because he's quick to check your mean ass?" I joke poking fun at her sensitive playing hard ass.

"No. But if you must know, Boy Wonder visited on the weekend tour Spring semester last year, and I was his tour guide. He was funny, and a hoot during the sessions so I invited him out to a kick back that Saturday night. He came, we kicked it, got drunk and ended up back in my room late that night. We got to messing around and things got hot and heavy between us, in the middle of our hot encounter, I got cold feet about my statutory shenanigans and stopped him in mid stroke.

Boyfriend was not happy and even tried to persuade me by gracing his face all up in the place if you know what I mean. He was ready and I put the brakes on him and mocked him for being too young and eager to understand my apprehension messing with a juvenile. He got pissed, got dressed and bit a hole in my air mattress before storming out my room! I had to sleep in my fucking car that night and make a mad dash to Walmart the next day after feeling myself sink onto the floor like I was sleeping on a bed of quicksand after that nigga left. While his whining ass was on the bus headed back home, I was researching how to patch the visible teeth holes I found in a perfectly good air mattress! Haven't heard from or seen his ignorant ass since until tonight." She spouts out mad like it just happened. When she finishes her story, I bust out laughing so hard tears start pouring out my eyes and I fall back up against the door. "Oh, so that's funny to you?"

"Uhm, hell yeah it is! The infamous pimp-stress herself got her caged rattled by an incoming freshman! Hell, yeah that shit's mad funny to me! What's even funnier is you thinking your issue with him has anything to do with me." I insist still chuckling.

"Fine laugh all you want but don't say I didn't try to warn your ass." She warns me following right behind me going back in the room.

"So, you just had to snitch about our night huh?" Dorian poses as soon as we come back in.

"Is that what you think it was…our night?" Destiny mocks him as she leans up against the closed door with her nose in the air.

"See that's the same shit that got your bed bit that night!" Dorian mocks of her right back and we both bust out laughing at her expense.

"While yawl giggling what's that glowing behind that door?" Destiny asks as she makes her way over to the closed closet door. My head instantly starts hurting the minute she notices it because I know she's not going to let it go until she knows what's up and I don't really want her or anybody else to know what's up.

"Nothing and that would be my business that you don't need to have your nose up in anyway." I say to her playfully turning her body in the opposite direction of the closet.

"Oh, but it's okay to let fresh meat in on the secret?" She antagonizes as she side-steps me and rushes back over and snatches open my closet door. When the almost blinding light illuminates the room, I know I am seconds from being totally busted.

"What the hell is all this?" Destiny asks in astonishment when she sees all the various plants set up under a strategic floor plan of fluorescent lighting for optimum results in my temperature-controlled closet. "Is this what I think it is?"

"Looks like a secret urban grow house to me E! You doing it up like that my Dude?" Dorian boasts excitedly. I quickly push the door back closed before answering either one of them although I know it's not going to stop the bum rush of questions. "Well, more like a grow-room.

"Watch your jokes Youngster. This is how I keep your ass herbal-upped."

"So, what you drug running for some bigger fish in town? Come on EJ you are too damn smart and privileged for that shit." Destiny asks still trying to get back in the closet, but I keep blocking her.

"You're right. I am too smart for that. When yawl puff with me you are not smoking no regular herb. My shit is of a special blend I cultivate personally. I run this shit for my damn self." I boast proudly to put them both on notice. *Ain't nobody about to risk getting kicked out of school, running no reggies around the yard. Tha fuck?* I think to myself.

"Yeah, but you come from money and privilege so why are you fucking around with this shit at all?" Destiny quizzes.

"Damn Deputy Dog shit! Look my dad has been preaching about the power of education since my sister and I were kids. My mother always pushed being an entrepreneur and generational wealth, so I took all their ideologies and smashed them together. I am

197

an agriculture major, and so I took what I learned, extended my research to cultivate my own marijuana strand that is all natural with no harmful sprays of pesticides and other poisonous shit. I grow it here and sell it to an elite clientele that keeps coming back. And now my boy, Dorian here is going to help me expand that clientele to make more ends. By the time I graduate next year, I will have a degree in this shit, industry job offers and a thriving legitimate grower's business. Why do you think I worked my ass off to get in as an intern in the greenhouse once Heritage became a testing site for the state's medical marijuana programs? I'm using my free education to get what I want without my parent's money or input." I explain in depth to both in an effort to dispel any myths they may concoct as to why I am doing this.

"Damn Dog that's heavy and righteous!" Dorian comments as I can see Destiny's wheels turning in her head without her saying a word.

"Well Des, what you got to say about my little business venture?" I pose thinking I am ready for any of her little critiques because I know she thinks she outthinks everybody.

"I'm thinking that I want in on your little marijuana shop of horrors here!" she says seriously with a hint of amusement.

"What? Girl please! I am already giving your pretty ass the helly discount on herb!" I protest.

"Well dis ain't dat Bro! That was one thing, this here industry is quite another. I know you don't need any more eyes on this little venture, so I am going to need a percentage for my silence." She offers coyly.

"You are seriously going to blackmail me Destiny?"

"If you give me a piece of the action Bro, I won't have to!" She insists.

"That's fucked up Destiny." Dorian adds in disappointment shaking his head from side to side.

"No, it would be fucked up if a campus administrator got some-kind-of anonymous tip about what's hiding in the closet. It may not point directly to you, but it could surely shut down this whole little money-making scheme."

"Damn girl, I'll give your ass 15% and not a penny more!" I surrender because I know Destiny well enough to know she will not let this go for nothing.

"Twenty-five percent and you have a deal."

"Twenty percent and that's my final offer." I protest as Dorian stares at us like he's watching a championship tennis match or some shit.

"Twenty percent and a $50 bag every other week and you've got a deal." She forces my hand even further.

"Fine...20% and half a Benjamin bag bi-weekly it is! Damn!" I relent finally frustrated as fuck as Destiny and I shake on the shit while Dorian looks on.

"Cool well gentlemen, I've got to get out of here. Maybe I can sneak in a few winks of sleep before today's homecoming events start later this afternoon. I feel like it's going to be a pleasure doing business with you EJ."

"It will for at least one of us Destiny. Now beat it so we can get back to our business." I encourage having had my fill of her shit already.

Once Destiny exits, Dorian and I continue working out the details of him putting me on with his gambling buddies. When we lock up and leave my office, right before daybreak, I have most of my strategy worked out. Although I agreed to give 20% and some puff for her silence, Destiny is not getting as much as she thinks. She has no real clue what I make so I will give her 20% of one of my deals. The rest will go in my pocket as it should. My girl will soon realize that she is not the only sharp color in the crayon box. I've got vision for days and my real work is just getting started.

Chapter 15
Bubble Bustin' is Hard Work
Dream

"So, since she worked us like field slaves last night, I'ma need you to run interference for me with Mom and Auntie Tina so I can handle some other business." I huff into my cell phone talking to my forever-needing-a-favor-from-me cousin, Destiny while driving a campus golf cart all over the Garden Valley area checking and replenishing all eight of the sanitation stations strategically scattered for the attendees at today's Welcome Home Chicken & Fish Fry on campus. It's a another socially distant, covid safety-procedure based spin on one of the long-standing traditional homecoming fundraisers and as the new First Lady and Events Director, this event is my Aunt Tina's and my mom, Kyla's baby.

"Girl I was the last slave standing last night! While your little busy behind was M.I.A. I am not trying to be back at it this damn early Dream. No way!" She protests adamantly but I am not having it. It's time for her ass to start returning a couple favors for a change.

"No Des I am already out here on duty handling the sanitation stations for Auntie Tina this morning, so I've got that covered. But if I am missing in action and being requested once the chicken and fish fry gets started just cover for me then let me know to get my ass back here. That's all. You can't do that little bit of shit for me as much as I cover your ass?" I hiss with much attitude.

"Okay, I've got you, damn!" She relents over sighs and moans, but I don't even care. That's what family is for shit. "But I better see your ass at that chicken and fish fry, and I am not playing!" She insists.

"I promise you will. Thanks, Cuz. I've gotta go. Duty calls."

"Yeah, well me too. See you later this afternoon right, Dream," She asks?

"Yep, you will Destiny talk to you later." I reply before hanging up.

Now that I've freed up a little extra time between tasks for the day, it's time to get to that other business that needs to be handled. I roll over to the newest honors dorm, Jordan Hall to check in on a reckless friend. I park the golf cart and make my way up to the fourth floor. When I get to room 422, I knock on the door but get no answer. Since its almost ten in the morning and there are no classes, I just know this dude has got to be in there. I knock harder. When I still get no answer, I look around first before doing the unthinkable. I turn the doorknob only to find it unlocked and slowly walk on into the room uninvited.

This room is a total mess. First, it smells like ba-dussy up in here mixed with shoe funk. There is left over pizza rotting on a paper plate on one desk and empty red cups that smell like cough medicine and grape soda, otherwise known as Lean next to it. There's also a nice size bud of marijuana nearby on the nightstand next to the bed. My favorite fuckup, Andre` is lying flat on his back passed out like a corpse with his broken arm glasses stretched across his face sideways and something sticky and stinky smeared across his right cheek and down that side of his neck. But the sight of my boy knocked out is not what wrecks me. Truth be told this scene has become all too familiar with Andre` lately which is how I knew to come and check on his ass. It's the sight of not one but two campus hood rats sleeping naked in the bed next to him that had me repulsed and fucked up. How do I know they are all naked? Because the blanket is barely big enough to cover Dre` and the sheets are jumbled up between the gruesome twosome chicks with the matted weaves offering up much T and A, for the world to see. This little nigga has been on a Leonardo DiCaprio Wolf of Wallstreet type binder for a minute and the shit is getting mad old, real quick. To get his attention, I begin tapping on his forehead since I need his ass to finally open the door of his mind to better decisions.

"Hey Fool, wake your sleazy ass up!" I yell as I tap hard as hell on his forehead. As soon as he opens his eyes, I go in. "Tell the bitches to hit the bricks!" I demand staring him down disapprovingly.

"What?" He asks groggily struggling to catch my hand so he can stop my tapping on his thoughts.

"You heard me Andre`! Tell the bitches to hit the bricks. They have got to go before your father, or worse, your mother makes their way up here looking for you!"

"Awl shit you're right!" He yells in a raspy hangover induced voice as he pops up like a jack knife and starts shaking the hoes awake. "Aye yawl gotta get up and go!" he hollers.

The chicks finally awake to his rude ass request, a far cry from his daddy mac vibes of the night before I'm sure and get their shit together for the quick exit without even acknowledging my presence in the damn room. Once they vacate like roaches when the lights come on, matted weaves and all, I get to the heart of the matter with my boy.

"What the hell are you doing Andre`?"

"What does it look like Dream? I'm trying to drag myself out of this damn hang over right now."

"That's not what I'm talking about, and you know it." I hiss to his stupid ass ultra-frustrated. "Why are you sabotaging your progress drinking lean and over-indulging in any mind-numbing drug your silly ass can find? Why are you running from your genius Dre`?"

"Because I don't want to be a fucking genius Dream that's why! I never asked everybody to make such a big fucking deal about my standardized test scores! I never applied for the scholarship that got me here, my scores on the ACT got me that! Now I'm here and everybody is putting all their high expectations on me, and I can't fucking handle it by myself all the damn time!" He shouts with a helplessness in his voice that I can tell he's been hiding for a very long time. In this moment, I can't help but feel sorry for him.

"So, you let the bullshit keep you company instead? Well how is that shit working out for you so far? Let's see, you look a mess, all stale, pale and stinky after your binder! Your grades are gradually descending into the toilet at warped speed. Oh, and let's not forget that your parents, who have been oblivious to your shenanigans because of their own issues thus far, are on campus and on the verge of discovering all your fuck ups in person! Or do you even care about any of that anymore?" I shout back at the top of my lungs in concern, trying to get him to understand.

"Hell no! I don't care if they find out! As a matter of fact, I want them to! Maybe then they'll act like they care about something other than one upping each other all the good damn time!"

"Dre` I get how you're feeling but this is not the way to get their attention. You are sacrificing your state of mind…" I resist.

"Yes, I am to finally coax them into minding their business…me…and our family!" He shouts as he breaks down into a full-blown cry, turning his back to me. I want to wrap my arms around him, but I can see he hates I am even seeing him like this…vulnerable and raw. Andre` is usually super smooth and cool for a sophomore his age, but not here and not now. When he finally pulls his faculties together, he makes his stand known with finality. "Look Dream, you are one of my…no fuck that you are my best friend and I know you're just looking out for me. But sometimes desperate times call for desperate measures and I need my parents help...desperately. Now you may not agree with how I am deciding to go about getting their attention, but I am not looking for your approval or permission. I am approaching my shit, my way and anyone who doesn't like it, doesn't have to watch me. They all can just look the other fucking way Sis and that means you too." He confesses with such seriousness that I know trying to talk reason to him now would be pointless.

One thing I've always admired about Andre` is once his mind is made up there is no changing it, even if it makes no sense whatsoever. Seeing that I am talking to the wrong person for sure about all this, I just lean in and kiss my friend on the clean cheek and turn to leave without saying another word because we all know that I will not watch him self-destruct right before my very eyes, no way, no day, and no-how. I vacate his premises with a new mission in mind. *Damn, I had no idea his shit had gotten this bad but now I see I've gotta figure out something to help save Andre from himself before it is too late.*

Chapter 16
Late Bloomers Are a Handful
EJ

On late mornings like this I love the fact that my family home is on the west end of campus. It does something for my ego to have so many dwellings I can call home or hiding spots at my disposal. But I keep it all in check because getting the big head is no good for business. I learned that lesson the hard way playing with my grades last year and almost lost my damn scholarship so, no, a brother has got to keep all his shit in proper perspective. That can also mean keeping up on things that don't even involve you directly sometimes, just like I'm doing right now.

I jog around to the back of the house in just enough time to catch my dorky-ass, too-smart-for-her-own-good, twin sister, Erin sneaking her lame-ass new dude out our parents' house in the middle of the morning. The look on their faces when the door opens, and he backs out through the threshold, still lip locked with my 6 minutes older, but still my baby sister is priceless. He turns around and BAMN! Leo-nerdo bumps his lankey, urban intellectual ass right into me. His glasses jump off his face as he struggles to get up off the ground after I push his ass to the side like a bathroom door.

"EJ what the hell are you doing here?" My sister yells all mortified the little nigga got knocked down.

"I live here remember, Erin?" I shout back with fire mean-mugging the hell out of dude.

"Ahh…no…you don't live here…Mom, Dad and I live here! Your ass lives on campus! So, what are you doing creeping around in the back yard of our parents' house?" She yells at me like I'm the intruder.

"You should be the last one talking about who's creeping! Now look here Erkel, I think you need to make your way back where-ever the hell your ass came from, like right now, don't you?" I suggest through gritted teeth to old boy once he gets his composure, tossing his book bag over his shoulder.

Old boy takes my advice and makes his way on to class, but not before tonguing my sister down in that doorway right in front of me. It takes everything in me not to knock his ass out for being disrespectful, but he's clearly not the one I need to be hollering at.

"So, ahh Twin when did this little junior-entanglement start?" I ask as soon as she closes the door, heading to the fridge.

"About four months ago," My sister blushes and that instantly tells me what time it is.

"Well, what do the parents think about him?" I inquire chillin' on the kitchen counter.

"Nothing because they don't know about him yet."

"Well, why is that?"

"Because this is all still new to us, and I don't want to hear everyone's opinions about it yet. I'm having fun just figuring things out for myself," she explains sweetly.

"Well then tell me, what have you figured out so far?" I ask with enough skepticism to choke a mule, but I'ma hear her out just the same.

"Well, for starters, he's smart and I am not just talking book smart EJ, he's worldly and street smart. He's ambitious and he's a guy that knows what he wants because he stepped to me! I didn't chase him, hell I barely even noticed him at first but come to find out he's been scoping me for a minute. Trying to work up the nerve to shoot his shot."

"I see…he's been liking you huh," I ask for clarity?

"Yes, and he is mellow just like me. He likes to just keep shit cool…not too heavy and I like that. I like him a lot."

"Okay you like him so much that you have yet to tell your family about him or invite him over for us to meet, huh?" I ponder still skeptical and not trying to hide it.

"I was gonna get around to it," she back peddles.

"When Erin?" I hound her.

"I don't know, one day soon…like after homecoming or at the end of the semester."

"Awl now you no that's a no go now that I know what's up! Why wait? Let's tell Mom and Dad tonight at dinner and see when they say it's cool to meet him.

"No EJ!" she protests adamantly.

"Why not Erin?"

"Because we are not ready as a couple for all that!"

"But as a couple yawl are ready to be naked frolicking around our parent's house fucking though?"

"Who says we're fucking?"

"No one has to say it with the used condom wrapper in the kitchen trash! Mom and Dad been beefing too tough to fuck lately, and I get mine outside the house so nobody can be busting it open up in here but you and boy wonder! So, miss me with the lies you're about to try to tell!"

"Awl Bro come on..." she offers defeated because we both know I'm right.

"Look, I am not feeling any of this shit so let's fix it. Invite old boy over to meet the fam."

"Not yet and contrary to popular opinion, you don't get to decide when he meets the fam, I do!"

Well, if you don't let the folks know what's going on with you and the cornball, I will."

"So, you gonna snitch," she screams in shock? "Why would you do that? This isn't even any of your business!"

"See that's where you're wrong Sis. Some corny dude has got my twin pulling freaky sneakies in my parents' house, and I'm supposed to just let him keep pulling the wool over my parents' eyes? No Ma'am, no ham and no turkey!"

"Seriously Bro? You do not see me inserting myself into your personal dealings so why are you trying to be all up in mines?" She whines like she's not six minutes older than me.

"Because you're sneaking and creeping which leads me to believe you've got something to hide, and if you don't then he probably does. If I'm wrong, then prove it. Let me know when Guess Who's Coming to Dinner will be here, and I'll be sure to be here with bells on. Now, if you'll excuse me, I have a very important presentation to get ready for so…"

"So…now that you're done interrupting my scene, it's all about you again, huh?"

"Something like that." I mock as I turn headed upstairs. "I will see my twin there, right," I ask?

"Yeah…unlike others I am clear on where my loyalty lies. Too bad you forgot."

"My loyalty is always with you Erin…especially when you just don't see it." I explain before jogging upstairs to take a shower, as she storms out the house fire-breathing dragon mad at me. I know she thinks I'm meddling but, I don't like seeing her be all secretive about some dude. That's not our Erin, and I know my dad wouldn't like it either but, he's got other shit to handle right now. So, that leaves the other man of the Smith household to handle the business of getting everyone on the same page, by any means necessary. When something needs to be done my mom says we should be like Nike and JUST DO IT so, that is exactly what I plan to do no matter who likes it or not.

Chapter 17
Saying Hello to Your Past
Cierra

As I look around this newly built greenhouse with a tropical rain forest feature of plants and flowers, I am amazed that my Godson, Eric "EJ" Smith Jr. is one of the master minds behind the project. Not only is this site a beautiful addition to the HSU campus, but its eco-friendly and operating under a sound, state-of-the-art underground water filtration system also created by EJ. Tina may have been worried when he decided to pursue a second major in Water Resource Management a year and a half ago but coupled with Agriculture, it's visible to everyone now just how EJ uses his passion and talent working together to make great things happen. In short, I couldn't be prouder if he were my own son and standing off to the side with Tina right now watching EJ's presentation, I can feel her delight.

"Can you believe your baby is responsible for all of this?" I whisper to Tina shielding my mouth with the event program.

"Just barely." She whispers back the same way as we both are sure to keep our heads and eyes facing the front. Although I see pride on my girl's face, her energy is off and that does not fit with this occasion, so I have got to see what's up.

"You alright Tina? Seems like your mind is 100 miles away right now," I inquire out of genuine concern.

"Damn Cee-Cee. It's crazy how after all these years, your ass can still read me like a book."

"Uh hmm, yeah that's what friends are for so, what's up with you?"

"Well, you know I support Eric even though we are not seeing eye-to-eye about how to best go about securing funds for the school," she explains as I listen intently after we casually make our way out of the greenhouse and into the beautifully decorated botanical garden outside, prepped for the Memorial Balloon Release tributing all lives lost during the pandemic from the university community at large.

"Right."

"So, I have taken the liberty to do a little research of my own on all the companies and individuals that are suddenly pouring money into our school programs. And this Gilliam Group is all over our school's growth and that is a serious red flag to me."

"How so Sis?"

"This guy, Chief Sheldon Ross, just appeared out of thin air all close to Eric and Cherod in the sake of Alpha and he was recently appointed to the position of COO of The Gilliam Group. Something seems fishy about all this recent abundance of supposed *support*." She explains suspiciously using air quotes on the word support to make her point.

"Well damn Tina what do you think all this means?"

"I don't quite know yet, but best believe I will figure it all out sooner rather than later. You can believe that." She professes seriously in a hushed whisper just as EJ's greenhouse presentation wraps up. When I look in Tina's eyes, I see a focus that reminds me of the old days when she flirted with journalism. My girl is about to get her Deputy Dog on and nothing anyone says is hardly going to stop her.

Following the guided tour through the greenhouse via the same path of EJ's water filtration system, attendees get to see his magic in action as water flows through a clear tubular structure further purifying the well water supply going into the greenhouse and garden. The tour ends with attendees being led into the garden where white tents are set up with white high boy tables scattered all around. Miss HSU is standing behind a microphone dressed in a white form-fitting, maxi dress with Andre`, Ananda and Anthony's son sitting next her in black slacks and a white button-down dress shirt. The boy looks urban sophisticated with his sleeves rolled to his elbows and his top two buttons undone, holding an acoustic guitar. An array of colors in flowers as far as the eye can see is the most beautiful backdrop for today's memorial balloon release ceremony and as usual, Kyla and her crew did the damn thing arranging this. When everyone is situated under the tents, equipped with either bubbles or a balloon the ceremony begins with Destiny singing an acoustic version of Tamela Mann's hit, *Take Me to The King*. I don't know what impresses me more, Destiny's singing or Andre's guitar skills? I had no idea he was artistically talented too.

"Wow he really does possess the very best of both of his parents, doesn't he?" I say ironically.

"I know right? I stumbled upon the info by accident, but once he got busted skipping my class for some head-on-head action, I was able to convince him to use his talents for good rather than evil." Tina jokes as we watch. Thank God I still have this program in hand to cover my face from revealing the giggles I'm trying to hide as she tells me all this.

"Well hell, I bet you could convince him to drink Jesus' juice after all that." I hiss still holding in laughter.

When the song is over, it's time for my speech and I smoked the fattest blunt known to man before sliding my dress on and twirling out the door headed here to cope with my nerves. I hope my prayers are answered because it is showtime and I'm so high that God's got it from here as I slowly make my way to the podium. I have my speech in my hand on index cards, but suddenly my nerves are screaming for me to just speak from my heart. When I first open my mouth, nothing comes out and for a slight moment, I panic. Then, I just take a deep breath and start again.

"When I was first asked to give this presentation, I wasn't sure if I could come up with the right words. Truthfully, I had a hard time figuring out what exactly the right words are. I now realize that there are no right words for what 2020 did to us all around the world. This pandemic gave us illness, fear and great loss and there are simply no words to make anything about any of that right. However, even in all the unfortunate circumstance this pandemic offered, somehow, in-spite of the pain, those of us who lived through it were brought closer together. Our faith may have been tested but hopefully never failed even in the face of loss and grief.

I made it through the first few months of Covid without being personally affected by the disease. I was in-the-midst of a communication crisis, or should I say stand-off with my mother, whom I was never really close to growing up. I grew up fighting for my independence and I stood strong in my convictions against the things she challenged me with, and in the end, we rarely saw things eye to eye. We didn't speak for four years and last summer, I ran out of time to fix things. She contracted the virus and passed away after two months on a ventilator, and I couldn't even visit her to fix things. And I am sure there are many here today that feel like they just ran out of time to make things right, to say I Love You or even goodbye. I stand here today offering the opportunity I am sure many of you, like me feel cheated of, a chance to say I love you and see ya later rather than a lonely goodbye. Those we lost will always have space in our hearts and will forever accompany us through the rest of our lives. I am still grieving but each day it gets a little better. Time surely offers grace in grief and when grief passes amazing grace is all that we will ever need. God Bless You and Us All.

Farewell Mama, I love you and I will see you again later! Amen."

At the turn of my last word, I release the dozen white balloons I'm holding and everyone in the garden does the same. Watching the sea of peaceful sentiments float to the clouds, grief I didn't know was there overcomes me. Leaving the podium, I find myself overcome with emotion as this marks the very first time, I have shared with anyone, anything about my mother's death.

I'm a mess by the time I get off that stage. An emotional wreak, I collapse right into the waiting arms of none other than the gentlemen I have come to know over the last few days as simply, Adam. His strong muscular arms catch me just before I drop out of the picture in the garden, and I have got to admit, crying into the broad chest of a fine, black man is never a bad thing. He simply holds me in place as I finally release tears, I had no idea were inside me still.

We stand in that tight embrace for what seems like an eternity before I loosen my grip around his neck first. When I look up into his eyes, I am captivated as he simply wipes away the tears from my eyes with his thumb. I back away completely embarrassed as he hands me a Kleenex. After gazing over his shoulder for a brief second, I see an image that I swear, has got to be an optical illusion. I squeeze my eyes together tightly and reopen them only to see what I thought I saw was gone. I shake off the confusion just as Adam speaks to me.

"Hey Eve, are you alright?" He asks sweetly seeming genuinely concerned about me.

"Oh yes, I am fine now. Thanks to you catching me. I would have fallen on my face had you not been here to rescue me."

"Well, it is always my pleasure to rescue a beautiful lady." He suavely responds as I am busy wiping the remaining tears from my face.

"I couldn't agree more." I hear another masculine voice say from behind Adam. When I slowly allow my eyes to focus in the direction of that last statement, I can swear my eyes are deceiving me again. But this time, the source is right in front of me alive and in living color. When we make eye contact, I am left totally speechless.

"Hello, Ms. Cierra Folsom. Long time no see," Gerald Tolliver, former HSU Band Director and my first love says to me flashing that same compassionate grin he possessed 20 years ago as all my motion, inside and outside stops.

"Gerald…" I utter slowly like I ride the slow bus. I can hardly believe my eyes, nor can I even begin to hide my shock seeing this man. We have a history between us that I haven't been able to shake for 20 years and now, he's here standing right in front of me.

"Yes, it's me. For a minute there I was afraid you didn't recognize me past this pesky grey in my beard."

"You're a hard person to forget." I let fall out my mouth without much thought.

"I can definitely say the same thing about you." He says casually enough but his stare into my eyes says so much more, and I don't know if anyone else can tell, but I can. It feels for a minute like no one else is in our immediate vicinity but Gerald and me. That is until others see a more immediate need to break this reunion up.

"Well Eve, if you'll excuse me, I see my party in the distance. Are you going to be, okay?" Adam offers to me who is now so preoccupied with Gerald's presence, I barely acknowledge he's still here.

"Sure, I'll be fine. Thanks again." I say somewhat dismissive in anticipation of what may come next with Gerald. I don't know what I'm expecting but for some reason, I know this is not just a mere coincidence. As Adam walks away, I do notice the mild look of disappointment on his face, but I'm sure he'll recover swiftly. Men like him always do. Left with a mountain of space between us now, Gerald and I just stare at one another for a few minutes before he breaks the monotony.

"Well, come on now. I know it's been a really long time but, can't I get a hug?" He asks innocently with extended arms. I smile and lean in. When our bodies touch why does a surge flow through my body like water? *I feel silly because I haven't been this close to him in decades so how is it that he can still have this effect on me?* It's familiar and awkward at the same time.

"Well, don't you look good. The grey is flattering." I offer trying to get my bearings together. *He smells so damn good. Better than I remember.*

"And you are still gorgeous. Aging flawlessly like I always knew you would." He compliments me with a sensual smile.

"So, what brings you here, homecoming festivities?" I ask making small talk to mask my attraction. *Damn I hope it's working.*

"That and I have family playing in the band this weekend." He pauses for a moment and stares at me closer before finishing, "My niece is in the band."

"Oh," I offer trying to stifle my relief that he said niece, "For a minute I thought you were gonna say your daughter or son is in the band." I accidently say without thinking. His eyes widen a bit before he finishes off my embarrassment.

"Oh no, no. Truth be told Cierra, I was never interested in having kids with any else but you so no, I don't have a daughter or a son." He says so casually serious that it leaves me speechless.

"Oh, wow I don't even know what to say about that."

"You don't have to say anything. Just know that it's true. Listen do you think we can grab a bite to eat or something and maybe catch up? I'd love to have a moment with you if I could."

"Sure Gerald," I hear myself say without hesitation and I want to smack myself for sounding so damn eager. "My schedule today is pretty tight though…" I say fumbling with my phone thumbing through my day's calendar.

"Whenever you can fit me in is fine as long as we talk." He says with another warm smile and that makes me even more curious as to why he suddenly feels the need to catch up with me.

"Okay, how about we exchange numbers and I'll give you a call later this evening to see if you're free?" I offer sweetly. He replies blurting out his digits and I quickly plug them into my phone and press send to call him back. "That's me so lock it in."

"That I already am Beautiful. Now I'll let you get back to your work and wait for your call. Looking forward to later Ms. Cierra." He flirts.

"Me too Gerald, me too." I offer as I watch him walk away, trying not to follow up behind him like the little lost puppy dog that I feel like.

"Ooh girl is that who I think it is?" Tina asks when she sneaks up behind me.

"Gerald Tolliver in the flesh, yes Ma'am." I say like I'm hypnotized.

"Damn he has aged delightfully. He looks better than he did when we were in school." She notices. "Are you alright?"

"For now, I am but he wants to talk and catch up later."

"What about I wonder?" She poses.

"So do I Sis, so do I," I say mentally running through every possible scenario in my head. *But I've gotta shake off that curiosity because I have got a practice to run, and too many more homecoming duties that require my attention to allow my anxiety to kick in over this. So, this unexpected trip down memory lane is just going to have to wait…at least for now.* I think to myself before getting back to work.

Chapter 18
Placating the Privileged
Eric

This week is moving faster than even I thought it would. We are already at the end of the week with the Miss HSU Coronation tomorrow night, and the parade and game on Saturday and I swear I don't know how the hell we all made it this far and with remnants of our sanity no less. Now it seems like the most important occurrences for this week like, the various Board/Trustee meetings, Hall of Fame ceremony and banquet, and fundraisers like the Alumni Chicken & Fish Fry, The Greenhouse & Botanical Garden opening all just flew by. Now here we are at the last big fundraiser in support of the diversity initiative, the Golf Invitational sponsored by The Gilliam group. I know my wife doesn't trust this company or its COO, Chief Shelton Ross Sr., but an Alpha Man is always a good man in my book. So, as tired as I am, I will muster up the strength to enjoy myself here because as much as I have allowed Shelton and his company to do for Heritage, playing the gracious host today is the absolute least that I can do weather wifey likes it or not.

Everything is going fine so far. My friend's fathers and fathers-in-law are bonding peacefully for a change and their wives seem pacified for the moment as they look on sipping lemonade as the men play a few relaxing rounds of golf all for a good cause. I'm out here schooling my boys, Cherod, Anthony and Chavon when I see some commotion brewing in the distance. *Fuck! I so do not need this shit right now!* I hiss out loud before I can stop myself. That's because I see a small mob of young folks gathering around some troublemaker over in the picnic area.

"What's going on over there?" Chavon asks sheepishly, squinting his eyes trying to see what's happening.

"Looks like someone's over there disturbing the peace to me, messing with one of the waitresses." Cherod answers him.

"Well, whatever it is this is not the time and damn sure not the place!" I announce as I begin making my way to where the unwanted action is.

The fellas follow me as I walk up on the disturbance trying with everything in me to keep my cool. But when I see my son, EJ and his friend, Dorian struggling with an unruly dude, it makes my head hurt and my blood boil. When we get closer, we see the culprit of the disturbance is none other than a totally wasted Andre` struggling to break free from EJ and Dorian's grip.

"Man let me go! I was just trying to talk to old girl! Yawl ain't gotta be grabbing on me!" He slurs loudly resisting their attempts to calm him down before we get over there.

"Man stop tripping. She's not feeling you Dog. Let's just go!" Dorian whispers loud enough for us to hear.

"No, I ain't going nowhere and if she ain't feeling me then let me hear her say that."

"I already told you that I've got a boyfriend. So, I'd say that means I am not interested, damn!" She shouts out in frustration snatching away from Andre's grip on her wrist.

"What the hell is going on over here and why does it involve my son of all people?" I hiss at the group through gritted teeth. Upon hearing my tone everybody stops in their tracks.

"Dad, I know it looks bad but trust me we've got him." EJ rushes to tell me as soon as he secures himself under Andre's drunken shoulder with Dorian holding up the other side for him. As they struggle with their boy, his father goes off.

"What the hell is wrong with you, Andre`? Where the hell did your under-aged ass get this smashed?" Anthony yells and it takes a pat on the shoulder from Chavon to get him to calm down a bit.

"I…I…ahh…" is all Andre` can manage to say before hurling all over the ground right in front of his seething father. The look of embarrassment on all our faces I'm sure speaks volumes to the boys.

"Oh, hell no!" Anthony yells and Cherod immediately steps into problem solver mode and Chavon and I follow suit.

"Ah sweetheart can you call someone to clean this up asap?" Cherod asks of the young lady Andre` was harassing. "Fellas can you guys get him back to his room to sleep this shit off?"

"Sure Unc. We can definitely do that. Don't worry Dad. We're gonna take care of him." EJ reassures us as he and Dorian practically carry Andre` off towards the parking lot.

"Well, I guess I'm gonna have to get with you guys later," Anthony announces turning to leave.

"Whoa, where are you going?" I ask Anthony truly confused.

"I'm gonna follow the boys back to their room to try to talk some sense into my son. That is if you don't mind Eric," Anthony counters talking down to me like I should know better than to question him.

"Ya damn right I fucking mind! Your kid shows his natural, black ass at a campus golf fundraiser and all your passive ass is going to do is try to talk some sense into him? Are you freaking serious?" I yell fed up with sugar coating the bullshit.

"Oh, and I suppose all-knowing-president Eric has a better solution huh?" He says in the most condescending tone he can muster.

"Hell, yeah I've got a better solution! Your ass needs to pop the titty out of that boy's mouth and quit coddling his ass! You up here offering stern talking-tos like some-kind-of-backwards time-out when he needs some grown-ass-man wall-to-wall consultation from his fucking daddy!" I snap and the looks on both Cherod and Chavon's faces lets me know I may have taken my own frustration a bit too far. Thank God we are a nice bit of distance away from the green where the event is still ongoing.

"Look, I have never been much of a disciplinarian type of parent like that!"

"Well then maybe that's your problem Bro," Chavon interrupts to stop me from taking shit from bad to worse, I'm sure. "Look Rod and I have got girls, so we had to find the softer side of parenting that worked best for our daughters, but I believe there is some truth to what Eric is saying Anthony."

"But yawl don't understand. When Ananda left, my son struggled. He struggled in school. He struggled at home. And I was all he had to lean on. He didn't have a mom, just me and I could never bring myself to punish him for that." Anthony explains.

"Dude, you're acting like Ananda was some deadbeat mother strung out of crack or something. She left to play basketball and sent you back the money, Dog! Keep it all the way real, okay? She didn't leave yawl destitute. She had him with her every summer and every other holiday so how did she abandon him? She may have left you, but she never gave up on her son and you know it!" Cherod counters looking Anthony square in the eye.

"Ant man, I think what the fellas are trying to say is that you have issues with Ananda because she left, and you have managed to pass those issues off to your son. The problem is you have also been overcompensating for him not having his mom 24/7 by giving him stuff over structure. Now he needs structure on a grand scale because he is acting out and fucking up and the only one that can correct his shit is you, my dude." Chavon explains with a compassion Cherod, and I don't have for him because it's causing us problems.

"Simply put, your way ain't working man. Don't you think it's time to find another approach before your boy fucks up something for himself for real?" I ask tiring of being diplomatic.

"I just didn't think it was fair for her to leave us like that." Anthony admits defeated. "I never thought she'd actually go and when she did, it was easier to hate her. But I never meant to give that to Andre` to deal with. I was just trying to soften the sting of her being gone."

"Yeah, but now his entitled ass is stinging you with his shit! This madness has got to stop and you, my friend, need to man up on his ass pronto." I advise with seriousness I know Anthony sees. "Now look, I'ma go gloss over this little situation and close out this event on a high note. But you all need to go holla at his seed as soon as possible. I don't need shit else hindering the remainder of this weekend's festivities." I announce before strolling off in the opposite direction.

Damn, I thought Tina and I had a lot of shit going on. Hell, we do, but at least we're married. Anthony and Ananda got a boatload of shit to resolve and they're not even a couple. I just hope they can get Andre` together before his antics get him hurt in real time.

Chapter 19
Seeing is Believing
Destiny

My coronation is tomorrow night, and it seems like no one gives a good goddamn except me. I've had to dip into my savings more than I intended to so, thank God the ladies have been racking in much cash over the last few days and especially nights. Thanks to them, I am happy to be making this trip to the ATM to put some of my money back into my account. When I pull into the parking lot, the line for the money machine is ridiculous so I decide to go inside to make my deposit instead. *My girl, Jazmeen is working today so I'm not even going to have to wait in line. I know she's got me.*

I strut into the bank on a mission when I notice my girl in the back corner of the lobby having an intense conversation with a familiar face. Surprised this duo even knows each other, I push my dark glasses further up onto my face and adjust my face mask to better disguise my identity. I then casually make my way over to the table nearest to the pair to fill out my deposit slip.

"Look, I am tired of playing with you! If you want another fucking dime from me, you better get that damn test! Because until I see proof, you ain't getting shit from me! Do you understand?" I hear the gentleman hiss at my friend with her arm pent between his and the wall. He speaks to her in a creepy ass tone that makes me nervous for her. So, I keep listening.

"I already took the goddamn test, but I can't control when the results come in! What about the bills I've got to pay now? You can't just leave us out to dry like this, can you?" I hear her plead in hushed whispers.

"I can and I will because this should have been handled like I wanted three years ago! If your skank ass would have listened to me then, we wouldn't be in this predicament now." He snarls close enough for the tips of their noses to touch as he throws their sorted past in her face. He stomps off in a huff once he's made his point and I make it my inconspicuous business to stomp out right behind his ass. *Ain't no way I'm gonna let talking to my roommate like that slide especially when she looks to hurt no one. She a good girl that's better than most so hell nawl I ain't letting her go out like that.*

I conveniently drop my keys as he passes by me in the parking lot and like the gentleman, he portrays himself to be, he takes the bait and stops to assist me, the stranger. He stops on the dime, kneels to pick the keys up, and extends them to me with a wide smile.

"Why thank you, Sir. I swear if I didn't know any better, I'd think you were following me." I say flirtatiously as a smile spread across his face when he sees me.

"Well, well, well…" he sings as he hands me my keys. "Fancy running into you here…"

"Yeah, well a boss' business is never done, I guess. By the way, that looked like a pretty, intense conversation you were having in there. Hope nothing is going on too serious?" I lead casually.

"Nothing that is really any of your business, Beautiful." He offers sweetly lightly brushing a curl from my forehead.

"See now that may be where you're mistaken. You see that girl you were talking to in there is a very, good friend of mines and when I see an elder all up in her face being overly aggressive, I'm going to make it my business."

"Oh, so you call yourself sticking up for your girl? What, you're a real ride-or-die chick huh?" He asks sarcastically. "Back off Beautiful, just because we banged doesn't mean I like that jealous girl shit. Neither of us has any claims in this." He whispers in my ear, gently stroking his index finger around my right nipple as he speaks.

"Don't flatter yourself Gramps! I just want to warn you about harassing my friend. This young woman is way more powerful around these parts than you may think." I counter through gritted teeth reluctantly smacking his hand down.

"Look Little Lady, warnings can get misinterpreted as threats and trust me, I am not the one you want to make threats to. Especially about things you only think you know." He warns seriously staring me down. Before I can reply another familiar voice calls out my name in the distance. Both of us looking in the direction of that voice, we see a very well put together older lady strutting her stuff across the parking lot, yelling and waving at me.

"Destiny…hey Honey over here. Fancy me running into you here. I was just stopping over here to transfer some money into your cousin's account real fast." Says my paternal grandmother, Gloria Turner of all people switching her mint green pants suit wearing self over to my car from her Chrysler 300. *Thank God for small miracles because little does dude know my Granny just saved his ass for now anyway.* "Oh, and I see you have already had the pleasure of meeting the new Dean of Students for Fitzwater, Hamilton Lang. Well, Hamilton this is my eldest granddaughter, Destiny Turner, the new Miss HSU come tomorrow night!" My grandmother boasts with pride, and I just want to throw up in my mouth, but I keep my composure in check. Sexy elder's eyes grow like saucers too slightly, but I don't think my grandmother even noticed.

"Yes, well we haven't been formally introduced until now but…it is very nice to meet you Destiny. Your grandmother has talked my ears off for weeks about her two beautiful granddaughters." He says graciously to cover his surprise.

"Right," I reply shaking his hand like we didn't fuck earlier this week. "Granny you're headed into the bank?" I say turning my attention to Gloria.

"Yes, I hate fooling with those ATMs, so I just go inside to handle my business. But I know I'll see you at the Board Meeting in the morning, right, Hamilton?" She says as she begins making her way towards the door.

"Oh yes, the Dean will be there with bells on indeed Mrs. Turner." He assures her with a smile. Once my grandmother is safely inside the bank, I know it's time to put Mr. Hamilton on notice.

"So, you're the new Dean of Students for Fitzwater huh? Funny how you never told me that's why you're in the area?" I say sarcastically.

"I say it's funny how you never asked who I was or why I was here. I didn't lie. It just never came up."

"Well, I am sure you'd also like the fact that you obviously had some kind of entanglement with a student as recent as about three to four years ago to never come up as well huh, Hamilton."

"You really need to stop speaking on things you know nothing about Beautiful." He warns me seriously. "If you want to keep up our little arrangement, you should keep quiet about spreading rumors."

"Well, if you don't want your little secret to get out, then leave my friend, Jazmeen alone. Give her what you obviously owe her and get the fuck on so no one gets hurt."

"Now what did I tell you about threats earlier Beautiful? I don't take to kindly to them Destiny. Careful now, you're fucking with a grown ass man here."

"That's good Hamilton because I don't issue idle threats. I make commitments and if my friend is bothered any more by the likes of you…I will blow your spot up like the World Trade and that…is no threat. Consider it a grown ass man promise. Now you have yourself the best rest of your day, ya hear?" I offer with finality as I close my car door, start the engine and pull off leaving him standing stuck in the parking lot. He has no idea who he's fucking with and hopefully he heeds my warning, that way I can keep fucking him from time to time and so he'll never have to find out how low I can really go.

Chapter 20
Where Friends and Foes Meet
EJ

Getting Andre's drunken ass back to his dorm room was not easy. This guy is out on his feet and smells like a mix of Jack Daniels and open ass! But Dorian and I are troopers wrestling with his ass all the way up to his room. After searching his pockets like SWAT to take his car keys, Dorian lets us into his room. Once inside we see an unexpected site that halts all of us in our tracks.

"Dammmmn…Man what the fuck happened to you?" Andre` announces as soon as he stumbles into the room, falling face first on his bed. When we focus in on his other roommate, Sheldon Ross Jr. trying to clean up the dried blood all over his face that's when we know another, more pressing issue has to be addressed. Sheldon is over on his bed looking ultra-lumped-up like Martin when he fought Tommy Hearns. He's messed up in a bad way. The brother has bruises and cuts all over his face and he's moving slow because somebody worked his body over good.

"Yeah, what happened to you?" Dorian asks.

"I got in a little altercation that's all…ouch," Sheldon answers in obvious pain as he struggles lifting his arm to continue wiping blood from the corner of his mouth.

"Ain't nothing little about those lumps on your damn head Man. You need to go to the Health Center to get that looked at." EJ suggests.

"Health Center my ass. Your crazy ass needs to hit the ER with that shit. Come on I'll take you, and on the way, you can tell me who did this to you." Dorian offers seriously.

"Man, that nigga's good just put a cold towel on his head and some ice or something on his lip because that shit is larger than life!" Andre's drunken ass slurs with a chuckle squirming around on his bed like a fish out of water trying to untangle his wife beater from around his neck.

"Oh, so now Andre` the Alchy has jokes." Sheldon replies.

"You shut your drunk ass up and try to sleep that shit off before your parents appear on the yard, and you need to listen to his drunk ass and go to the ER!" I interrupt the two stooges to get on with my day because contrary to popular opinion, this Rescue 911 shit was not on my itinerary. "You take Dre's car and get him some assistance please."

"And you'll stay here and keep an eye on him?" Dorian asks pointing at Andre` who is now passed out on his pillow.

"Who? I know you don't mean me? I'm about to hit vendor's row and get myself something to eat. He's gonna need a minute to get it together after he wakes up and I have got shit to do. My good deed for the day is done." I announce with much finality.

"Well, that's not entirely true, Son." A deep, husky voice growls from the hallway right before the fella's dorm room is invaded by one big ass dude, and his slightly, bigger and much more-scarier friend. Their presence seems intentionally intimidating and it is working like a muthafucka. They bust into the room like they own the whole damn building.

"Now tell me who the hell did all that damage to your grill?" The shorter of the two giants barks to Sheldon.

"Ah come on man. I can handle my own shit." He answers shaking his head in resistance.

"If that was true, you wouldn't be sitting here with your ass whipped like cream!" The Big Man barks back. "Now who the fuck is responsible for this shit?" He shouts.

"Yawl gotta excuse his rudeness but in case you haven't already guessed this is my father, Sheldon Ross Sr. and my uncle Reed Ross.

"Oh…nice to meet you both. I'm Dorian, Sheldon's roommate and this is my friend, EJ and over there is our other roommate, Andre`."

"Hey fellas, see ya fellas. I need to have a talk in private with my, Son." He hisses in a low threatening tone.

"No…I got myself into this, and I'ma get myself out of this. And Dad you can't be throwing people out of their rooms here. They have just as much right to be here as I do." Sheldon insists between winces trying to sit up straight in the bed.

"Now that you mention it, how did you get yourself into this situation anyway?" His father yells.

"That's my business Dad." He attempts to stand firm but can't and falls backwards onto the bed.

"Well, the way you do business got you fucked up, so tell me what you've gotten yourself into voluntarily, or I will just have to find the answers on my own. And you know how resourceful I can be, Son."

"Damn…gambling, okay? That's what I've been doing to make my ends, gambling."

"What? As much money as I give you your greedy ass done started gambling now and that got your face bashed in? What's the damn ticket Sheldon?" His father shouts with nostrils flaring. When his face turns pink, I am sure he is gonna bust a blood vessel.

"That's not important."

"The hell it's not! If that were true, your face wouldn't be looking like that dog with the black
bull's eye around your damn eye, and a busted lip among other things probably. Now quit stalling and spill it!"

"Ten thousand." He mumbles with his head down.

"Ten Thousand?" Both Dorian and Sheldon Sr. shout in disbelief.

"How the hell did you get caught owing that much? I just play around with a little Blackjack. I never get in deeper than that." Dorian admits.

"So, you're the one that introduced my son to this mess?" Sheldon's dad asks.

"Look I just showed him how I made money to pay my tuition by gambling on the Dark Web, but I never told him to get in over his head like this!" Dorian explains passionately.

'But I was winning, and someone invited me to poker game where the pot was crazy high, and I was killing it at first…" Sheldon Jr. explains passionately trying to get his father to understand.

"And then the shit went left and before your dumb ass knew it you were ten stacks under, right? Isn't that how it went, Son" he asks sarcastically as its obvious to all of us he already knows how it went down.

"Something like that. Now I don't quite know what to do because they caught me coming out the café and I never saw it coming."

"I'll tell you what you're gonna do. You are gonna go to the hospital and get checked out like your boys suggested, while I clear your debt. I am sure they are not playing games with you, so I'll handle that." His Dad explains more calmly.

"Well, we'll help by getting him to the hospital." Dorian offers kindly.

"That's nice but you will do much more than that after turning my son on to this wayward behavior, much more."

"I don't understand. What more can I do, Sir?"

"Well since you like giving leads so much, just like you turned Sheldon Jr. on to making money on the black web, I want in on what you make. I'm sure we can come to a fair percentage agreement."

"Oh no see I usually work alone."

"Good so I won't have to keep up with other folks in order to get my cut of whatever you make. Less work for my contribution."

"What contribution?"

"Tell me this, Dorian, is it? Do you think the university would smile upon your methods of making money on their campus? Especially after I explained how you got the son of one of the university's biggest contributors in bed with loan sharks and bad people? How would all that info work in your favor?"

"I don't think that info getting out would work in my favor, Sir. I think it could get me expelled from the university instead."

"Funny because that's exactly what I was thinking so to answer your earlier question, I think my silence about this little situation is the best contribution from me that you can get. Don't you?" No one has to ever know as long as you say our arrangement is a go."

"How much?"

"Let's see I want to be fair so, let's just say 40%."

"What??? That's almost half!" Dorian shouts in   outrage

"Almost half beats none doesn't it?"

"Yes, I suppose but..." Dorian replies defeated.

"And it also beats getting beat the hell down worse than he is now figuratively, of course." Boss Ross interrupts aggressively whispering in the young brother's ear in a way that scares me from across the fucking room.

"Right," Dorian repeats with Mr. Ross to demonstrate he gets the message.

"Now you get your ass up and let me get you to a doctor. My people won't ask as many questions as the hospital will. You know what I'm saying?" Mr. Ross demands as he directs his brother to help his son up. As they head to the door, Sheldon Jr. doesn't even look at me or Dorian as he passes us with his head down, and tail tucked between his legs like the little bitch he is. If it wasn't for his ass, none of this bullshit would even be happening.

"It was nice meeting you fellas," Mr. Ross says as they leave. "My son will get me your contact info and trust...you will be hearing from me soon Dorian." He announces with a sinister smile right before slamming the door shut. When the immediate threat is gone, we're left to figure out our next move.

"Now this muthafucka is gonna try to pimp me and take half my shit! What the hell am I gonna do? Bro I make money to send home

262

to my sister's foster care family. I don't just do this shit for myself!" Dorian yells hysterically.

"I don't know Bro but please believe this is not over and Mr. Ross ain't as much the Boss as he thinks he is. I don't know what we're gonna do, but let him hold you by the balls, damn sure ain't gonna happen. Not on my watch." I promise him as we make our way back to my hide-a-way spot to work out a plan of action.

Chapter 21
What You Don't Know Might Hurt You
Jazmeen Henry

When I get back to the apartment, I am shaking like a stripper, all messed up over my confrontation with Hamilton. *I can't believe I've managed to get myself caught up like this. Amateurs do this type of shit, not supposed-to-be-Pros like me. I know better than this shit. I do now, and I did back then too.* I think to myself as I undress in my bedroom, still shaking. *Come on now Jazzy, you've gotta get yourself together because the school bus will be here dropping your son off from day care in nothing under twenty minutes.* I say in my head as I take one long deep breath after another. No one will be happier when those damn test results come in than me. Finally, this charade will be over. A good ten minutes into my peace, my crazy ass roommate, Destiny comes storming all up into my solitude, fucking up the vibe, quizzing me like Columbo.

"Girl, are you alright? How long has that Hamilton dude been harassing you? Don't worry I got his ass straight. He won't be bothering you anymore, I bet you that." She professes confidently. I can't begin to know what the hell she's talking about.

"What? Hamilton? What are you talking…"? I stumble over my words as she's talking a mile a minute.

"Don't even try to deny it Sis. I saw you two at the bank earlier this afternoon and it looked like he scared you out of your mind. So, I confronted him with the fact that I know a test will soon be deciding his fate. I let him know that I've got pull around here and he had better leave you and your son alone. Or else his reputation will come under back draft I'll create so much fire!" Destiny announces like she's the answer to my prayers when in truth, she's really letting me know she's ignited a nightmare.

"You did what?" I hiss in shock.

"You heard me! I let his ass know that somebody's got your back and he's not gonna get away with ditching you or trying to make you disappear if shit doesn't go his way!" She reiterates to prove she's done a good thing.

"You have no idea what you've done Destiny! Why did you have to say anything? This is not your business!" I shout in raging anger.

"I was trying to help you! If that man fathered your baby, then he needs to step up and be a fucking father!" She yells back at me.

"Yes, but he's not the only one who could be the father! And that, my little sister, causes the fucking dilemma here."

"He's not? Well, who the hell else could it be then, and do they know?" She asks in disbelief.

"All you need to know is he's a very powerful man, that I can't afford to be playing with Destiny and neither of these guys take kindly to threats. They eliminate them instead." I assure her already thinking I may be telling her too much. But I have been trying to handle this shit on my own for three fucking years and look where it's got me. Maybe another eye on the situation can give me some clarity on what to do.

"Okay I know about Hamilton, so who's the other man, Jaz?"

"Sheldon Ross." I say with my head lowered in shame.

"Sheldon Ross Jr, really? Oh well, I mean he's a little too young, wild and free for my tastes but fuck it he was grown enough to bone so..." Destiny rationalizes in dismissal as she keeps talking.

"Sheldon Ross Sr!" I yell to drown out her rambling. She stops in mid-sentence and just stares at me. "But little Cory is three years old. That would have made you 17!" She shouts after doing the math in her head.

"Actually 16½ when we had our encounter. I was a wild girl back then and I was no stranger to doing something strange for the change."

"Sis that's statutory rape." She says in disbelief.

"Not if I was tricking at the time and had both dudes at once. I was fucked up yes, but the orgy was consensual, and I got pregnant. That's what happened. I lived in denial damn near until I delivered, and everything was good. My mom and I handled shit, and I didn't look back. Until Cory got diagnosed with a rare kidney condition, and my mom unexpectedly died. Her insurance helped to pay for my baby's medical bills for a long time but then he had to go on the donor's list. That's when I knew I needed to find his father. And now that I've found them, they're stalling. Your little threats aren't going to make them come around and play nice. These are the type of men that play for keeps. Their end game is to end the damn game, okay? Now one of them knows that you know too much! You have no idea what you've managed to get yourself into Destiny!" I cry because she is in too deep already and if I know my friend, Destiny, that's just the beginning of our problems.

Chapter 22
Long-Awaited Confessions Revealed
Cierra

"Wow I can hardly believe that in a few short hours, your baby niece is going to be crowned Miss Heritage State University, Kyla." I say as we wrap up the finishing touches to the decorating of the main auditorium for tonight's coronation. It's been a busy week, but it's been epic just the same.

"I know right? It's more than a dream come true Cee-Cee. This right here couldn't have been better if it was written." She agrees with tears in her eyes.

"Crying already Kyla? Girl you better get yourself together. There's gonna be plenty of time for tears later tonight." I joke as I poke fun at my overly emotional friend. And why shouldn't she be emotional? Her family is still doing big things, so she has the right to be proud and a bit weepy.

"I know but as I compare the feelings I have now with all the regrets I had about giving birth to Dest...I mean about the baby I lost when Destiny was born and now seeing her and all she's grown into...it just makes me think, you know?" She stutters as quiet tears drip from the corners of her eyes.

"I remember how that loss affected you then but look at how it all turned out. Destiny is flourishing and your baby, Dream is just that. Your personal little Dream come true."

"Yes, a Dream come true that seems to have it bad for Ananda and Anthony's boy, Andre`." She admits with a chuckle. "The irony is crazy right?"

"Yea but knowing them both personally, I can see it. Dream can be good for Dre`. Her clear thinking should level his spoiled ass right out. And his go-getter spirit will wake up her quiet inner beast, just watch." I explain.

"Yes, but I fear her getting serious about a boy too soon will take her mind off the prize. Distraction can be deadly, Sis."

"She'll be fine, Sis. She's got you for a mom, remember? You will never let her steer too far off course." I reassure my friend as our little moment is interrupted by a visitor I have been waiting on pins and needles to see.

"Well, well Mrs. Chavon Turner is that you?" I hear Gerald Tolliver ask my girl as he enters the auditorium and struts confidently to the stage by us. With each step he takes toward us, my heart beats harder.

"Oh my God, Mr. Tolliver as I live and breathe! How are you?" She greets him with a big smile and a huge hug.

"I haven't seen you since your anniversary party two years ago." He reminds her as they hug.

"I know…it is really good to see you again." She agrees pleasantly.

"Ready for tonight?" He asks.

"Yes, my entire family is on ten excitement level wise. We are all very proud."

"I can only imagine. Hello Ms. Folsom." He greets me finally after releasing my friend.

"Hey," I greet for lack of anything else to say. *I can't believe he still makes me speechless this way.*

"Well, if you two will excuse me, I've got pre-coronation business to handle. I'll see you both tonight." Kyla says before exiting stage left, right on queue. When she leaves, my throat grows dry as the desert and my heart drops to the pit of my stomach. *Yes, I am aware that I asked him to meet me here, but now that he's standing in front of me, I don't know what to say or what I expect him to say.*

"So, you picked the auditorium for this little meeting huh? How befitting." He says calmly staring at me.

"Yea well, I've been so busy this week, it was either here or nowhere as it seems my business is always somewhere on this damn campus nowadays." I joke nervously.

"Cierra are you nervous?" He asks kindly slowly stepping closer to me.

"A little." I whisper.

"Why? I'm not here to hurt you. I just need to say some things to you." He explains cautiously stopping when he's directly in front of me, eye to eye.

"Like what Gerald? After all these years, what could you possibly have to say?" I ask exasperatedly tired of playing the cat and mouse game with this man.

"Well," he starts but stops in mid-sentence and just stares into my eyes the way only he can. "Damn… as much as I have gone over in my head again and again how I was going to say this to you…now I just…I just…" he pauses.

"You just what, Gerald?"

"I just can't stop myself from wanting to kiss you right now Cierra and it is driving me fucking crazy!" He admits like it is killing him but taking one step even closer to me. With my head down, I am instantly afraid to look into his eyes.

"Am I wrong for not wanting to stop you?" I let fall out of my mouth before I can even stop to think about it.

"As wrong as it is for me wanting to do it. I really never thought seeing you again would affect me like this." He says passionately touching me with his words and sentiment that is all over his face right now. It's the type of emotion and vulnerability that most men try to hide at all costs. But not now, and not Gerald.

"Like what?" I ask panicked to know where this is going. He's got my full attention.

"Like I still love you, Cierra! But I do! After all these years woman, I still love you!" He confesses with an urgency than cannot be faked. He's out here buck naked emotionally and so am I.

"And always has!" I hear a female voice say in the distance from the back of the auditorium. When she appears from the shadows, it doesn't take an introduction to know who this mystery woman is. Her voice has too much boom to be a mere acquaintance.

"Valencia! What are you doing here?" Gerald asks with annoyance.

"Awl Gerald honey, I am here to hear my husband confess his love to the woman I have been trying to emulate for the last 18 years!" She announces with attitude. "So, you are the infamous Cierra Folsom huh? Well, it is nice to finally be able to put a face to the name that has haunted me in and out of my marriage for years. I am his wife, Valencia Tolliver." She greets me matter-of-factly as she extends her hand to me. I shake it as I stand totally shocked this shit is even happening.

"You are so wrong right now Valencia." Gerald growls lowly to her through gritted teeth.

"No, you are but what else is new, right Gerald? Look I just came to let you know that I have signed the papers, okay? I am okay with letting you go. No more fighting to keep a man who clearly does not want to stay, right? Look, you have been a wonderful father to my daughter and even a fantastic husband but this thing between you and I, has been over for a while now. And…we both know it. It's time to get to the business of living the rest of our lives, don't you think?" She explains. As she speaks his and her faces soften. I am floored at the maturity she's displaying. If he were my husband, I don't think I would let him go so easily.

"I never meant to hurt you, Valencia." He admits.

"I know Gerald, but we have hurt each other too much already pretending so now it's time to let go. Here…is my olive branch." She says handing him a manilla envelope. "You are finally free my guy. Be good to yourself." She says before kissing his cheek and turning to leave. She looks back at me. "Be good to him Cierra. He has been waiting a long time for you." She says pleasantly with a single tear falling down her face as she goes back in the direction from which she appeared. When she leaves, we stare at each other in total silence for what seems like an eternity.

Without words he reaches his hand out to me. And in this moment, I am so scared to accept it because of what it means. Am I ready to try this love again? Am I mature enough for his love now? Is he sure he wants me, or is this some mid-life crisis type shit for him? A million questions run through my mind at warped speed, but nothing is strong enough to stop me from walking into my destiny and his arms because I am still to this day in love with Gerald Tolliver. Always have been and always will be, right or wrong…that is my truth and finally it is his too.

Chapter 23
Clearing Up the Blurred Lines
Destiny

I can't believe the day of my damn coronation has to start with me playing Captain-Save-A-Hoe, more literally than figuratively for one of my most trusted incognito escorts. Truthfully, I don't mind being pulled away from the Covid Vaccination rally site this morning especially when I'm assisting the one and only Mr. Chance O. Devlin, our resident campus Mr. All-That-And-A-Big-Blunt! All the women want him and those who have had him are like Busta Rhymes screaming, *Gimme Some Mo*! He's not overtly attractive although his Hershey-colored skin is flawless. However, what he lacks in looks, he more than makes up for in style and charm.

Did I also forget to mention Chance is one of the most expertly groomed brothers I know that ain't flaming that is? His grades are first rate, and he is a graduating senior and new member of Alpha Nu Alpha Fraternity. So, around these parts, he looks connected like Verizon. And, although Chance comes from humble beginnings, he puts in more work than most at all he does. That's how he got Mr. HSU! Nobody works harder than Chance. He also has a secret he works even harder to keep, and nobody knows that, but me. We've become real cool over the years so, when I came into his backstory, I promised to keep his secret, if he covered my ass every now and again. He agreed and we've been partners in the status game around Heritage ever since.

We teamed up and campaigned together for Mr. & Miss HSU and the campus ate our shit up. It started like a couple's campaign, but when I caught Chance with Rico on his knees in their dorm room accidently on purpose, I could not let that charade go on. So, we staged a big public breakup, and makeup as friends to continue our quest for the campus top spots as singles just running together. Plus, it made my stock as a grown ass woman go up to befriend him after hurting me. He's no limit just like me so our shit, is always put together with a purpose. That's how we do and that's why I am out here picking his ass up from an outing. Yes, he could have simply called an Uber, but no…boyfriend just had to call me.

When I get to this hotel, motel too dingy to be a Holiday Inn, I am reluctant to use the room key to go inside. It's a bit too run down looking for my tastes. I don't think this joint has any stars, but hey it ain't my party. It's Chance's wild ass that's got me here so let me just get myself together and go get him. I call his cell and get no answer which annoys the hell out of me. So being short for time and patience, I decide to bust up his party and go inside the room.

As soon as I get a good four steps into the room, the door slams shut hard behind me and that's when I feel an arm reach around my neck and squeeze. My heart sinks to the pit of my stomach as I struggle to get free. The more I resist the tighter their grasp gets, and it doesn't take long for their strength to overpower mines. Once my movement slows down my assailant whispers through gritted teeth into my ears.

"Look little Bitch! As you can see, you are not the only one who can get info on folks and use it to their advantage. You keep throwing around threats and you might end up getting your own little operation some unwanted exposure. You know what I'm saying?"

"Oh, so is this where I'm supposed to be all scared, crying and begging you to keep my business quiet? Because if it is, I'm gonna need you to come better than that. See I think statutory rape of underage students, trumps my supposed slut barn. What do you think?" I hiss back with much sarcasm. I don't scare that easy.

"Little girl you better be real, careful with who you choose to play games with around here before you find yourself in too deep."
.
"Well, you've got info and I've got info. Let's see who's story they gone believe first." I challenge like I'm not scared out of my mind. I am…scared shitless in fact, but I can't let this person know that.

"If I didn't have strict orders, I would do your smug ass myself." My assailant hisses in my ear with mild rage as their grip get even tighter around my neck. I was supposed to ask where Chance is and what's his part in all this because I definitely got a text from him on my burner phone, but my fear makes me forget all about that shit.

"Well then you need to let me go then, since you can't do shit else with me!" I shout getting right back to struggling to be let loose. That's when I get hit upside the head with something hard and I stagger back when I feel my attacker let me go. All I see is a blurry shadow, as I fall to the floor hard. My head is ringing, and I hear voices, but can't make out what's being said. I feel my body being picked up by two people. One has my legs and the other had me under my armpits. When they throw me in the car, the trunk slamming closed is loud enough to make me head throb like a tooth ache and that's when everything around me goes black.

I don't even know how much time had passed when I wake up. All I know is I am in my room back at my apartment, fully dressed, still groggy and in desperate need of an aspirin as my head is bumping where I got hit. I can feel a nice size lump where the pain is. I check my purse, which is lying next to me, and all my money and credit cards are still there, making me breathe a short-lived sigh of relief. I remember what happened and I was terrified, but all my boasting must have made an impact. That's why they knocked me out and dropped my ass off back here. *I knew they wouldn't want any of the smoke I bring with me. Didn't they know they were fucking with a real one?* I brag out loud as I get a sudden burst of energy. I don't know what happened to Chance's ass or how he is tied in with this shit. But right now, I ain't hardly got time to be investigating that shit. *Today, is still my day and no one is going to steal anymore of my time or my shine on this here day!* I profess loudly once more before heading to the bathroom to commence getting on with the rest of my day. That means pampering myself to the fullest starting with a long, hot shower, then, calling Dream to have her meet me at the auditorium to help me get ready for my coronation. *You see nothing and no one is going to ruin this day for me. Today the spotlight will be mines indeed as I am officially crowned Miss Heritage State University above all else!*

Back to the Present ...

Chapter 24
Chaos at the Coronation
An Angelic Perspective

From the time Destiny's lifeless body is discovered on stage in the center of the spotlight, until the paramedics takeoff with her the scene is straight chaotic. With frantic levels at an all-time high, somehow Eric springs into protective mode and immediately gets security and campus police to clear the building. Within minutes, the local police are all over the place and news crews have even started setting up shop. Tina instinctively and expertly handles the media like the pro she is to support her husband and protect his legacy as well as her own. A totally panicked Cherod Turner reluctantly sends both his wife, Kayla and sister-in-law, Kyla with Cierra to see about Destiny. As much as he wants to accompany his wife to see about his daughter, the father in him needs to know what the hell happened to his baby between him leaving her before her entrance and now. Since he knows he can't get that at the hospital, he stays and confers with the police. Chavon, Anthony and Juan also remain to support Cherod, Eric and Tina. Life may get in the way with the crew sometimes, but in times of need everyone steps up and plays their position. That's just how family does.

"Okay President Smith, the campus police and armed security have finally managed to clear the auditorium. The local police have been given the go ahead to move in to investigate the crime scene." The Captain of HSU Police reports to Eric over his trusty two-way radio. He never does any campus event without one. That's also how he was able to radio an ambulance for Destiny so quickly.

"Okay thanks, Roger that," Eric responds with Cherod breathing down his neck in panic.

"What the hell is taking the police so damn long to get here, huh? I need some answers and I need them now!" Cherod shouts one step from losing his grip as he rants and raves. Everyone looks on in shock because what does one say to a man who's just saw his daughter stabbed and bleeding during what was supposed to be a glorious occasion?

"Calm down Cherod." Eric replies calmly and it sets Cherod off further.

"Calm down? How can I calm the fuck down when my daughter has been assaulted? Fuck you mean calm down?" Cherod shouts back at Eric so enraged Anthony deems it necessary to step into the space between Eric and Cherod in case Cherod jumps.

"Look acting a fool up in here right now isn't gonna get shit accomplished! So, Eric is right, Cherod. You need to calm the fuck down. Somebody's gotta keep a leveled head around here man. Come on back now, we need you Bro." Chavon preaches to his terrified big brother in efforts to level his spirit. We see it visibly working as the immediate tension dies down as the police bum rush the scene.

No more words are spoken as the men and women in blue do what they came to do. Within minutes, they have the stage taped off, with investigators all over the auditorium collecting everything that could be evidence. Eric shows the investigators into the dressing room area where Destiny was last seen before the coronation, and the rooms where everyone involved in the event were held. There is so much going on that it's hard for any of them to keep up. When the detectives get on the scene things get even more serious and real. A short, slender frame fair-skin woman with red curls prances on the scene with authority in dark sunglasses and a matching mask covering her face. Wearing a blazer and jeans with her badge around her neck, everyone can tell she is all about her business and when she speaks for the first time that sentiment is confirmed.

"Around what time was the assault discovered," she asks the investigators.

"Around eight in the evening Detective," the investigator replies.

"And was the victim conscious upon discovery?"

"That's a negative. She was bleeding from the abdomen, with her wrists bound and unresponsive."

"And what hospital was she taken to?" The detective continues too official and formally for Cherod's tastes and he lets it be known.

"What the fuck is up with the 20 questions huh Detective? While you're in here playing jeopardy and shit, my daughter's attackers are probably long gone! So, why don't you get your Johnny-Come-Lately ass out there and find them?" Cherod shouts as the fellas attempt to calm him down once more. Eric speaks up in his friend's defense.

"Please excuse him detective. It was his daughter that was attacked. You understand."

"Yes, I do, wholeheartedly," she replies calmly before turning her attention back to Cherod. She slowly takes down her dark sunglasses as she addresses him. She begins speaking before she raises her head.

"Sir I should have started off introducing myself, I'm Detective Davison-Dexter and..." she says nonchalantly until she focuses in on who it is she's talking to. "Cherod?"

"Hayley?" Both Cherod and Juan ask out loud in unison.

"Cherod Turner, oh my God this happened to your baby? Jesus! I am so sorry family! It's been years!" She says when it registers that these people are more than just victims at a crime scene. These are her people. This girl that was attacked is her sorority sister's baby and niece so this here situation has just been upgraded from serious to personal. As Hayley serves up warm, engaging hugs to Cherod, Chavon and then Anthony. When she and Juan are face-to-face for the first time in months, she stops short of an embrace with him. His disappointment is evident.

"Hayley, Sis I need to know what happened to my baby girl!" Cherod explains frantically. His eyes are full of tears and his facial expression is pleading for her to give him answers.

"I know Cherod, and you know I am going to do everything in my power to get that info for you, but you have to leave room for us to do our jobs. Fussing, cussing and raising hell is not going to get us any closer to finding out what happened. The police and my team of investigators will get the justice your family deserves. Now, do you trust me?" She explains in the calmest tone.

"Yes, Hayley we know we can trust you." Chavon cosigns for the group.

"Good. Well, I think you all need to get over to the hospital. I am sure Kayla and Kyla are beside themselves with worry. They need you all over there with them. I will make sure the police and investigators handle all business here, and then I will meet you all at the hospital with updates as soon as we have some." Hayley encourages to a much calmer group. "Cherod, I know you're upset but, you have got to keep your emotions in check. Kayla and Destiny need you to be the leader you are. Now is not the time to fall apart. Destiny is going to be fine, and we are gonna get the folks responsible for all this, I promise, Bro."

"She's right man, let's get you all over to the hospital." Juan suggests to his boys while staring his ex-wife down the entire time. As the fellas head out the auditorium, Juan takes his chance to speak to her.

"Detective…wow? I didn't know you got promoted."

Yeah, it's been about 7 months now but I'm finally getting used to it." She replies pleasantly without looking in his eyes.

"You know it's good that you got here when you did. He was a mess before you got here. No one could calm him down." He explains sweetly.

"Well, that's normal in circumstances like these. He's not a businessman, or a board member here…he's just a worried father. I get it. I can't believe this is even happening. How is Kyla dealing with all this?" Hayley asks matter-of-factly still without eye contact or emotion.

"She's a mess of course. That's her niece. I'm just glad you're here and handling this case." Juan expresses sincerely.

"Yea, me too."

"You know I miss seeing you, Hayley."

"Juan please…this is not the time…"

"I know that, but I can't help still loving you."

"Are you really doing this right now? We are divorced Juan."

"Not because I wanted to be! Please just talk to me." He pleads. He grabs her hand, and she snatches away.

"When I get more information, I will meet them at the hospital…" she dismisses his last request like he never said it.

"Really? I haven't tried to contact you in months, no phone, no email oh and definitely no visits, but baby you're here now and our family is in crisis, and I'm supposed to act like all this shit is normal?" Juan shouts in frustration as Hayley starts to walk away from him.

"No, this shit is not normal, but this is the way shit is and you can't be mad when it was you that made shit this way! Now if you'll excuse me, I have work to do, and you do too. Our friends really need you." She offers dismissing all Juan just said to her before turning her attention back to the scene. Juan just stands speechless as he watches her walk away. He knows how much her job means to her and in these circumstances, it means even more, and he knows that too. Her pot shots hurt, but he's tough enough to handle her worst and he's nowhere near done, even if Detective Hayley Davison-Dexter thinks she is.

Chapter 25
Truth in the Fear of Tragedy
An Angelic Interpretation

Over at Tri-County Regional Hospital the uneasiness, and all out fear of an entire family are front and center as the waiting room fills with all the people who love Destiny Turner. Her mother, Kayla is silently weeping, rocking back and forth with a piece of her daughter's bloody Miss Heritage State University sash that was obviously severed during her attack, still balled up in her hands. Kyla, Destiny's aunt is sitting with her sister on one side, rubbing her back as she too has a constant flow of tears streaming down the sides of her face, and her own daughter, Dream on the other side of her gripping her mother's hand tightly as if she's a new, toddler trying to walk all over again. Kyla's mumbling something under her breath as she tries to comfort both her daughter and her sister, but no one can make out what she's saying. The assumption is she's praying to herself as their mother, Jacqueline looks on in horror at her daughter's dismay while holding hands with Destiny's other grandmother, Gloria Turner. The patriarchs of the brood, Michael Mansfield and Rasheed Turner are just returning with hot cups of coffee for all, hoping to hear an update soon on their granddaughter's condition. Although they have mastered the concept of courage under fire, fear and anger still sits in the pit of their bellies over this situation that neither of them, possesses the ability to control.

Dream put in a text to Andre` and when he woke up out of his drunken stupor, he linked back up with EJ, Erin and Dorian after the news spread like wildfire all over campus. As if the dark cloud this mess is going to put on not only homecoming, but on Heritage State as a whole, isn't enough to worry a student to death, Dream's thoughts quickly drift to the cousin she loves like a sister, in there fighting for her life. Just when she thinks she's not gonna be able to hold back a breakdown, Erin and the crew rushes through the Emergency Waiting Room doors just in time to catch Dream's collapse. As the boys greet the elders, they all are forced to just sit, helplessly and wait for news.

After about 2 more grueling hours, Cherod, Chavon, Ananda and Tina storm the

Emergency Room entrance in panic. As soon as Kyla sees Tina, she rushes past her husband, Chavon and into her girl's arms and sobs on her shoulder. Chavon just looks on and shakes his head as he throws up his hands in surrender. Cherod and Kayla embrace and cry trying to console one another as everyone else looks on. The ladies quickly alert the guys that because Destiny has lost a lot of blood, she's going to need a transfusion. Kayla urgently tells both Cherod and Chavon to go to the lab and donate asap as both she, Kyla and both sets of grandparents have done already. As the men rush to do as they're told, Hayley breezes in through the sliding doors.

When Kyla, Tina and Ananda all see Hayley for the first time in 17 years, it's all just too much to handle. Without words they all rush each other; hugging, crying, and trying to comfort each other. Once they all are able to somewhat compose themselves, Hayley is forced to get back to business. After hugging both sets of grandparents, as well as Kayla and Cherod, her detective protocol takes over.

"Now we have collected a major amount of evidence, but I feel like I should get your statements now, before things get even more hectic later once the doctors come out," Hayley explains calmly.

"Sure, but I don't know what more I can tell you. One minute she was fine, beautiful in fact, and ready to make her grand entrance. And then she was…" Kayla's voice tapers off as she breaks down again and Cherod quickly wraps an arm around her shoulder.

"Hayley that's really all she knows. Hell, that's all any of us knows!" Cherod shouts in frustration.

"Well, we have what we belief to be all her belongings left in the dressing room adjacent from the auditorium entrance. That includes her purse, the clothes she changed out of, a duffle bag, a jacket and a minute phone. Those things are on their way to the evidence room as we speak. Hopefully, we'll have some leads and possibly some answers soon. When I left the campus, my team was checking her car too." Hayley informs the group. "Don't worry we're going to do all we can to get whoever did this."

"Thanks Sis," Kyla says to her friend as she fidgets with nervous energy. Hayley notices but shrugs it off. After all Destiny is Kyla's niece so she clearly has reason to be upset.

"No problem, I'm going to go see if the doctors have any more info for you. Sometimes it helps to know people who know people." Hayley offers kindly before heading to look for Destiny's physician.

While everyone else is camped out in the waiting room seemingly in their own world's, Kyla is getting more and more antsy by the second. She's graduated from fidgeting to full out pacing back and forth, mumbling inaudibly to herself. If people didn't know any better, they would think she's the one with a daughter in Emergency. Suddenly, Hayley reappears with one good looking ebony doctor following in light blue scrubs.

"Hey everyone, this is Destiny's doctor's intern, I told him I knew where to find you all." Hayley explains as Kayla and Cherod rush to speak with the intern along with everyone else.

"Okay, what's our daughter's condition?" Cherod quizzes the man without so much as a handshake.

"And you are," The intern asks?

"You heard me say she's my daughter so that makes me her father, Cherod Turner!" He shouts angrily.

"Oh, my apologies Sir," the intern continues as he checks papers on his clipboard before speaking again. He looks like something isn't matching up as he scratches his head still reading the paperwork. "And who is Destiny's mother," he asks?

"I am, Kayla Mansfield-Turner. Now enough with the damn third degree! Are you going to give an update on my daughter's condition or what? We've been here fiddling our thumbs for hours now! What does a woman have to do to get some information about their child around here?" Kayla rants at the top of her lungs and instantly the intern is taken aback. He keeps looking from Cherod and Kayla back to his clipboard, flipping paper after paper, going over what looks like chart after chart without saying anything at first. But when her outburst reaches streaking levels, the medical professional losses his cool.

"Well, with all due respect Mrs. Mansfield-Turner, the first thing a woman has to do is prove maternity to get information because according to these lab results, I have here…Destiny Turner is not your daughter!" he spits back at her like two-day old chewing gum, and it hits the target hard.

"What the fuck did you just say? Someone get me a fucking real MD over here stat! This boy has lost his damn mind!" Kayla screams.

"Son, you must be mistaken. This is my wife and that girl in there, Destiny Turner is our little girl!" Cherod insists.

"Sir, can everyone who gave blood donations in the lab this evening raise their hands?" The intern requests. Destiny's parents, grandparents and Aunt and Uncle all raise their hand. "Well, I hate to be the bearer of unexpected news but the information we have here says that Kyla Mansfield-Turner and Chavon Turner are Destiny's biological parents, so I can only offer information about her condition to them!" He spits back in a nice-nasty tone that hushes the entire room. "We are going to need you all to sign off on treatment forms for Destiny immediately."

Everyone is stuck in shock. Kayla looks at her younger sister with helplessness she has never experienced before. Cherod is shell shocked and even Chavon is tripping off this news. The only one that does not seem surprised by this startling revelation is Kyla. And everyone wants to know why she's not surprised.

"Baby what the hell are they talking about," Chavon says to Kyla and Kayla says to Cherod at the same time? But before anyone can say anything else, another, more esteemed medical professional emerges to speak to the group.

"Excuse me, I am looking for the family of a Miss Destiny Turner please?" He announces loudly in the packed waiting room. As soon as her name is mentioned all heads turn in his direction.

"We're her family Doctor," Jacqueline Mansfield speaks up for the group.

"Well, I am so sorry to inform you that Destiny passed away just moments ago. There was just too much blood loss and nothing further we could do. I am so sorry," Before the doctor can finish his statement, streaks of agony can be heard all throughout the room coming from Kayla.

"Oh God NO!" Cherod shouts as his 6'4" frame breaks down to the floor. Chavon just hugs his brother as he too cries. However, when Kyla goes to comfort her sister, Kayla unleashes her wrath.

"Get the fuck away from me! Tell me what the hell you did Kyla! Why did that man say that Destiny isn't *my* daughter? Why did he say she's *yours*? What did you do, bitch?" Kayla screams as she rushes Kyla right there in the waiting room of the hospital. The grand dads intervene before Kayla can get to Kyla as everyone is beside themselves with grief. Pandemonium erupts within the Turner/Mansfields' families, and everyone wants answers to the same set of questions.

First, who's really Destiny's biological parents, Kayla and Cherod or Kyla and Chavon? Second, can the university and this progressive affluent family survive the scandalous circumstances igniting fires all around them? Lastly, who was mean, vindictive and vicious enough to pick homecoming as the scene of a murder on the yard? This hot story is just getting started as we await the novel chronicling the aftermath of this situation one detail at a time in the follow-up installment, Murder of the Yard Part 2 coming soon by Authoress, Tracie E. Christian on B Cyde Books LLC.

Reader's Roundtable
Discussion Questions

Thank you for reading Murder on the Yard – The Black College Sabbatical 20 years later. In an effort to keep the black college conversation going please see the following Discussion Questions for your next book club or reader's roundtable meeting! Enjoy!

1. How do you think Eric's decisions & subsequent plans for the University will be impacted by the events of Homecoming?

2. Who were you most surprised to see still tied to Heritage State University?

3. In a post-pandemic era would you attend the first Homecoming since reopening the country?

4. Which event captured your attention most?

5. Whose drama do you think is the most serious?

6. Which student has the most to lose on campus?

7. Which set of parents needs to check in asap?

8. What damage-control measures do you believe the university should take in the aftermath of the coronation?

9. What do you think Kyla Mansfield-Turner is hiding and will her sister, brother-in-law and sister ever be able to forgive her?

10. Who do You think killed Destiny LeLani Turner?

11. If you have read the original Black College Sabbatical series, how did it feel to revisit all the original characters and storylines? Explain.

Check out more B Cyde Books Selections
At www.thebcyde.online